DATE DUE   J1310

The Top-flight
Fully-automated
Junior High School
Girl Detective

The Top-flight Fully-automated Junior High School Girl Detective

E. W. HILDICK

Illustrated by
Iris Schweitzer

DOUBLEDAY & COMPANY, INC.
GARDEN CITY, NEW YORK
1977

ISBN 0-385-08259-2 Trade
       0-385-08328-9 Prebound
Library of Congress Catalog Card Number 76–42337

Contents

The Top-flight
Fully-automated
Junior High School
Girl Detective

1

A Very Special Occasion

It was very unusual for Alison McNair to spend so much time over her appearance. For one thing, she was basically too impatient. If anything was worth getting all dressed up for, she usually couldn't be bothered to waste time over preparations. She was usually much too busy either (a) deciding what she would do and say when the time came, or (b) looking at the clock and willing its hands to move around faster.

And for another thing, she was usually far too conscious of the fact that with her thick, long red hair and large brown eyes she could get away with wearing anything (even when it conformed to the school dress code!) and still look pretty good.

But on this particular evening the circumstances themselves were very unusual, and for two hours she had been trying on, and flinging off, and retrying and reflinging in different combinations, all the clothes she had—including one or two items her mother hadn't yet missed from her own wardrobe. And not only was Alison concerned about her personal appearance in all this, she had also even found time to criticize her kid sister Jeannie's attempts. In fact it was all so hectic that when Jeannie kept coming in from her room and saying, "How about *this*, then?" it was sometimes difficult for the younger girl to know whether her sister's snapped-out opinion was meant for Alison's own appearance or Jeannie's.

"Too cluttered!"

"Too formal!"

"Too sloppy!"

"Too dressy!"

"*Too* casual!"

This confusion arose because Alison never turned from the mirror to give her verdict. She would just continue to stare fiercely at her own image with Jeannie's in the background, and sometimes she didn't make herself clear until Jeannie stumbled into the wrong move. Then she would snap:

"No, not you, you dummy! Come back and let's take another look at you."

Or:

"Well, go on then! What are you waiting for? Go and change it. It makes you look like some old Kewpie doll that got put in the washer by mistake!"

And Jeannie would then just sigh and do what she was told. She had red hair, too—every bit as bright and thick as Alison's—but she was much more patient. Besides, this really *was* a big occasion, and she didn't want to spoil it by having one of her rare fits of stubbornness and starting an argument with Alison that would only waste time. The clock on her sister's

2

dressing table kept reminding her that eight-thirty was drawing nearer and nearer, and she knew how important it was to look right, to get—what was it that Alison kept calling it?

"The perfect image!"

At last Alison said it again, but this time with a note of satisfaction.

"Me, Ally?" Jeannie asked hopefully, glancing at the clock, which now said eight twenty-five. "Or—or just you?"

"Both of us, my sweet!" said Alison, turning around for the first time.

Jeannie blinked. This "my sweet" bit was something new. It was rather like Alison calling her "my pretty" that time they were practicing witchcraft. She wasn't sure she liked it, but at least it showed that Alison meant business and was putting everything she'd got into this new role. And that promised a very exciting future.

"But—" Jeannie was still not sure. She glanced down at her own dress and back at her sister. "But mine is so different. I mean—"

"That's the *point,* love!"

Jeannie blinked again as Alison turned back to the mirror with a fiery shimmer of swirling hair. This "love" was another new term the younger girl looked like having to get used to.

"Perfect!" Alison was saying. "Casual elegance. With just that touch of formality provided by you to set it off. . . . Hey, look at the time! Come on, stupid, or we'll be late!"

And on that more familiar sisterly note, they hurried out of the room.

Now a stranger looking in on this scene might have wondered.

What *was* the occasion to cause all this fuss and excitement? Was it Alison's birthday, a party?

Nowhere nearly right. It would be months yet before Alison made fourteen.

Jeannie's birthday party then?

The answer to that would have been: "Don't make us laugh! What? Alison McNair get so excited about a *kids'* party?" Besides, Jeannie had had her eighth birthday already, just a few weeks back.

Was it something to celebrate the start of the Easter holidays then? Like a dance?

Alison's own response to that would have been short and scornful: "We don't dress up for *dances!*"

Visitors, then? A visit from some special relatives?

Again Alison's reply would have been scornful— though tailing off into wistfulness perhaps. "None of our relatives is *that* special. . . . Unless maybe it was Uncle Ray, back from Hong Kong." (Uncle Ray was the young, handsome one.)

Well a visit *to* someplace then? Was *that* what they'd been preparing for? A theater? Hey, yes—a first night on Broadway?

And this time Alison's eyes would have glowed and Jeannie would have giggled. This was the nearest yet, though it didn't involve a visit to anyplace farther than the sitting room of their apartment.

"A *television* show?"

It wasn't a stranger but their brother Tom who bleated this out as they walked in: Alison rather unsteadily on her new platform wedges, shimmering from head to foot in her sequin-studded denim pants suit, and Jeannie demurely, in black patent ankle-strap shoes, white knee socks, and the green velvet dress with the yellowish lace collar—not her best, but the one that she liked best.

"You mean," said Tom, still staring out of round blue eyes, "that you're all got up like this—like—like Christmas trees—just to watch television?"

He was eighteen and, like all brothers that age, he *was* something of a stranger to his younger sisters, when you came to think of it. Certainly they never let him in on any of their secrets.

"It's a very special show," said Mrs. McNair, taking pity on him. "That's why."

She herself had been let in on this particular secret, if only to make sure that the girls had first claim on the color set that evening between eight-thirty and nine-thirty.

"Special?" Tom scratched at his already tousled hair. (Fair, not like the girls', not even like his mother's, which was sandy.) He looked baffled, slightly annoyed. Like most big brothers who pretend to be so uninterested in their sisters' activities, he really couldn't bear to feel that he'd been left out of things. He flipped through the pages of *TV Guide*. "What's so special about"—he glanced at the channel number lighted up on the set, then back at the book—"about yet another episode in some crummy old police drama?" Then his face changed, went harder. He looked up. "Hey, Mom, I wanted to watch the hockey play-offs on NBC, not some stupid—"

"Then watch it on the portable in your own room."

This was Mr. McNair, speaking quietly but firmly,

5

his glasses glinting over the top of his newspaper.

"But the portable's only black and white, and—"

"This is *very* special," said Mrs. McNair. "Why don't you tell him, Alison?"

"Because we're—" began Jeannie.

Alison restrained her sister with a languid, elegantly casual hand. Languidly, elegantly, casually, she sat farther back on the couch and crossed one elegantly shimmering leg over the other. Her voice too was languid, casual, and elegant—the voice of one of her favorite actresses:

"Because, sweetie, we happen to be *in* this show, that's why!"

"Yeah!" said Jeannie, not half so casually, and wriggling into a more comfortable but very inelegant position, sitting with one leg doubled under her and the other waving about with excitement. "So now sit still, Old Tom—uh, sweetie—and watch nice and quietly. Or we'll not give you our autographs."

Tom ignored her. He was still staring at Alison.

"Oh, come *on,* now! Who d'you think you're kidding?"

Alison didn't deign to reply. She was looking at her watch. The commercials were being screened already.

"She's *not* kidding!" said Jeannie, fiercely gloating. "We *are* in it. Me and Ally and Emmeline!"

"Where *is* Emmeline?" muttered Alison. "She said she'd come to watch it with us."

Tom sneered. Now he did turn to Jeannie.

"This is a police drama," he said. "Not the Three Stooges!"

"It's true, though," said Mrs. McNair. "They happened to be over on the West Side, visiting Emmeline's aunt, when one of the scenes was being shot."

"Yeah, and we watched them, and the cameras were pointed at us, O.K.?" said Jeannie, scowling in triumph at her brother.

Mrs. McNair was looking almost as excited as her younger daughter now, as the last commercial jingled to an end. She said:

"And Emmeline's father knows someone at the network and he says this week's episode is *the* one. The one with the West Side Highway car chase in it. The one they watched being filmed."

Then the titles came up, and the crashing menacing chords of the signature tune filled the room, and Tom's head jerked to the screen, and Mr. McNair put down his paper, and Jeannie squirmed, gurgling with anticipation.

For the first time, Alison lost some of her cool.

"Where *is* Emmeline?" she murmured again, glancing impatiently back at the door.

2

The Big Scene

The visit mentioned by Mrs. McNair had taken place several months earlier, toward the end of the previous summer. Emmeline had been asked by her mother to take some freshly baked brownies to her sister—Emmeline's Aunt Beth—and Emmeline had asked Alison and Jeannie to go with her.

They had agreed readily. They had been to Aunt Beth's many times before, and it had its attractions.

For starters, it was a pleasant journey through the park, on a crosstown bus, with not much walking to do at either end. (An important consideration on a day that was so hot and humid that the only clothes the girls could think of wearing were their shortest shorts and lightest shirts, despite the special nature of the occasion.)

Then there was Aunt Beth herself. She had been a fashion model. She was still very thin (which was why her older sister was always sending home-baked goodies across) and she was sometimes willing to talk to the girls about her modeling career, a subject Alison always found interesting.

Best of all, though, was the apartment building where Aunt Beth lived on the tenth floor. It was a new one, with a balcony overlooking the West Side Highway and the Hudson River, and (irresistible to all three girls) it had a TV monitoring system in the lobby, with a battery of screens on which the doorman could watch for the safety of residents and visitors in the elevators and corridors above.

"Let's hope it's Miguel," Emmeline kept saying, on the way there, her round, placid face shining with anticipation.

"Ooh, yes! Let's!" said Jeannie, squirming on the bus seat.

"So why don't we all cross our fingers?" said Alison. "And *keep* them crossed. All the way."

And she watched with fierce intentness to make sure the other two did just that.

For Miguel was the doorman who let them perform. While he and two of the girls watched the appropriate screen, the third girl would go up in the first empty elevator and act a part. They would take it in turns to do this for the whole of the ride to the top, which was twenty floors. They had a pact with Miguel that if anyone else got in they would quit acting, so as not to cause any complaints—but it was rare for anyone to join the elevator on the upward journey once it had left the first floor, and it usually worked out fine.

Thus Jeannie had given her solitary displays of what she thought of as ballet dancing, varied with simple acrobatics. ("Making up in vigor what she lacks in grace," as Alison once expressed it, in her role of lobby critic.) And thus Emmeline had given endless variations on her two favorite dramatic studies: The Fisherman's Wife Waiting on the Harbor after the Storm, and The Removal of the Bandages after the Operation on the Blind Girl's Eyes. ("Miss Grant has a feeling for tragedy, but she could stand to lose a little weight," was one of Alison's less severe criticisms of those performances.)

As for Alison herself, she put on the most elaborate acts of all, often playing no fewer than six different parts on a single journey from lobby to penthouse. Her crowning achievement had been a complete play, devised by herself, entitled *The Drunkard's Reward* and subtitled *A Drama in Twenty Floors*. In it, she had played the parts of the staggering drunkard, the worn-out wife, the brave but beaten daughter, the pitiful grandfather, and the soldier son, back from the wars, whom everyone had believed to be killed in action.

It had stunned the watchers into complete silence, leaving tears in Emmeline's eyes, a perplexed frown between Jeannie's, and a strange dancing glitter in Miguel's. But Alison didn't really care about their opinions. It was her dream that someday a big Broadway producer would enter the building and be stopped in his tracks by what he saw on that lobby screen.

"My gosh! Who *is* that girl? Quick—get her name and phone number! We've got to have her under contract immediately!"

Well, it had never happened yet. And it wasn't destined to happen on this particular afternoon, either. Miguel was not on duty. They had given themselves pins and needles in their crossed fingers for nothing. What's more, it wasn't even Chuck, who *occasionally,* on a *very* quiet afternoon, let them have one combined dramatic ride, which was never much fun because then there was none of them left down in the lobby to witness the performance and report back.

Their faces fell when they saw who *was* on the door.

"Uh-huh . . . it's Frank!" groaned Emmeline.

"Just our luck!" said Jeannie.

"Leave him to me," said Alison.

She put on her sweetest smile.

"Hi, Frank! You're looking good. You must have lost twenty pounds since we were here last."

Long experience with people who tended to be plump (like Emmeline, and Mr. McNair, and even Tom) had taught Alison that this was the way to charm them into doing special favors. And Frank the doorman did more than tend to plumpness. Frank, frankly, was fat.

But it didn't work. Not on this hot day.

"Yeah?" he said, mopping at the sweat that had collected around the brim of his uniform hat. "So I'm not planning to lose any more weight, fooling around with the TV. This is here for security purposes, not screen tests. . . ." He glared at Emmeline. "Your aunt know you're coming? . . . O.K., then. On your way. I'll buzz her now."

And that was that. There was no arguing with

Frank when he was in that mood—which was nearly always.

Nor was it much better in the apartment. Although Aunt Beth made them welcome and thanked them, she obviously had no time for reminiscing.

"I have some important letters to write," she explained. "But there's no need to rush off. Why don't you all help yourselves to a Coke and go sit on the balcony. Help yourselves to some of these brownies, too. . . ."

So they did. And that's when things began to take a turn for the better.

"Hey!" squealed Jeannie, spraying crumbs and Coke onto the balcony rail. "Look at all those *people!* On the *highway!* They'll get *killed!*"

"Don't yell with your mouth full," said Alison. "She's right, though," she added in a lower tone to Emmeline, as they stared hard at the scene below.

A whole stretch of the highway, from the Seventy-ninth Street exit down, was thronged with people. People on foot, that is, or on bikes—but not one of them in a car. Some were simply strolling along. Others were running: not *across* the highway, but *along* it. There were two or three joggers and, in one place, a whole bunch of little kids who were having sprint races under the supervision of a young man, using a section of the three northbound lanes as running tracks. There was another group busy tossing a Frisbee to one another over the central reservation. There was an old lady on a tricycle. There were some older boys on skates, and one very agile girl on a skate board, weaving in and out of them all.

12

And there was even a man with a set of drums—a complete kit—sitting there practicing, bobbing and stomping and slashing and sending the clash of his cymbals swinging across the steamy, polluted atmosphere, through the rush and roar of the diverted traffic down on Riverside Drive, and up to their balcony, ten stories high.

Emmeline was laughing.

"Don't be stupid, Jeannie! This part of the highway's been closed to cars for weeks. They say it's unsafe for all the usual traffic and it's been scheduled for repair."

Alison nodded.

"I remember seeing something about it in the news the other day. What I like about the West Side is the way the people make use of something like that, when they get the chance."

"Yes," said Jeannie, feeling a bit put down by the older girls, after her genuine cry of alarm. "But they're being moved off *now,* anyway. Look. Those policemen."

"That's strange," murmured Emmeline, frowning. "I wonder what *that's* about?"

Jeannie had been right this time. Two, three, four cops had suddenly appeared and were busy ushering the people off the highway: strollers, joggers, skaters, cyclists, sprinters, Frisbee flingers, everyone—including the drummer, who, after giving one thunderous roll of defiance, was now busy packing up his kit.

"Spoilsports!" growled Alison. "The people weren't doing any harm!"

She felt angry enough to go down and stage a sit-in, right then and there, as she stared at the suddenly empty lanes.

"I bet it was nice and cool there, too," said Jeannie. "So near the river and all."

She said it with one eye on her sister, knowing Alison well, and hoping her words might spark off something explosive, something revolutionary, something exciting.

Emmeline was more placatory.

"Oh, there must be a good reason for it, though. I mean *surely*. I mean—yes! Look!"

All at once, two police cars had come speeding up the entrance ramp at the far side. Hardly slowing for the maneuver, they each made a lurching U-turn on the highway and went north along the southbound section for a couple of hundred yards. There they stopped, paused, and slowly turned again, facing the way they had come. Then they stopped again, but the drivers remained behind their wheels, alertly crouched, as if waiting to race into action once more.

"Something's happening down there!" said Alison, leaning forward to get a better look.

Her voice had lost its indignant tone now. She had caught a glimpse of something moving behind the bushes that screened the ramp: something moving slowly at first, something yellow. Then:

Crack!

It sounded like a pistol shot. A puff of blue smoke arose from the bushes. The yellow movement became a blur.

"It's a cab!" cried Emmeline.

She was right. It came hurtling onto the highway at an even greater speed than the police cars.

14

"And there's another car right behind it!" cried Jeannie.

This was an ordinary brown sedan. But it had a red flashing light on its roof.

"An *unmarked* police car!" murmured Alison.

"Oh, and look at the other two now!" said Emmeline.

The blue-and-white police cars had leaped into action. Already the first one had overtaken both the brown car and the cab, with the second one roaring up close behind the others. Then, with a squeal of brakes (echoed by Jeannie), the first police car pulled over in front of the cab, causing it to stop abruptly, hemmed in by the brown car at its side and the second blue-and-white car behind.

Cops jumped out of both patrol cars and crouched with their guns drawn and aimed at the cab.

"Hey—just a minute!" drawled Alison. "Do you see what I see?"

She was referring to the uniforms of the men who'd jumped out of the two cars. They seemed perfectly regular from the waist up—hats, dark blue shirts, badges, and so on—but below that they were wearing what looked like brief blue denim shorts.

"Those aren't—"

But she was cut short by another squeal from Jeannie and a gasp from Emmeline.

"Look! Ally! Just look who it *is!*"

Emmeline's voice was an awed whisper.

And Alison turned from her inspection of the crouching figures and gazed, first at the man who had got out of the cab, hands in the air, and then at the figure that had emerged from the brown car.

15

It was this last one that Emmeline had been so excited about. And there was no mistaking it, even at that range, even with his hat on: the figure of the Great TV Detective.

"It's—isn't that—?"

Emmeline broke off with a gulp.

Alison nodded.

"It's him all right!"

It was the way he walked—shoulders hunched, hands in the side pockets of his jacket, very bulky, yet seeming to glide, to float, so graceful were his movements.

And, confirming all this, the scene suddenly broke up, with everyone relaxing and the "cops" holstering their guns, and the man from the cab lowering his hands, then taking off the white straw hat he was wearing and mopping his forehead with the sleeve of his dark blazer. Another bunch of people emerged from the bushes, one of whom seemed to be very much in charge, talking and waving his arms about.

"That's the producer, I bet," said Alison. "They're filming a scene for one of next season's episodes."

"Gosh, yes!" said Emmeline. "But it's not right yet," she added hopefully. "You can tell by the way he's pointing and shaking his head."

"They're all going to do it again!" said Jeannie, as the men began to get back into their various vehicles.

"You bet!" said Alison. She'd read quite a lot about the pains taken by TV producers. "And they'll be doing it again and again and *again* till they get it all right." She began to sound quite ferocious, as if she herself were in charge of the production. "I mean that was sloppy, just sloppy!"

Then she remembered herself and realized what a stroke of luck it had been.

"Hey, come on! What are we doing up here when we could be down there? Let's take a closer look!"

So they had gone down, scornful of the doorman and his mere ordinary foggy little security TV screens now, and out across the street and under the highway to join the crowd behind the cameras at the far side of the ramp. They were just in time to witness the conference after the second run-through— and to suffer a bitter disappointment.

The man from the brown car wasn't the star after all. It was someone very much like him in general build and mannerisms, but now they were close to him, they could see that he had a thinner, younger face.

"That's only the stand-in!" said Alison in disgust.

They were just behind a real cop, with real uniform pants: one of the men who'd helped to clear the highway and were now busy keeping the crowd of onlookers back. He must have heard what Alison had said, because he glanced at her and nodded.

"Yeah," he said. "That's the stand-in, right enough. He sweats it out until everything's set up perfect. Then the big man himself comes along in his air-conditioned Cadillac, all nice and cool, for the final take. That's the way to earn your dough, right?"

He was sweating and looking with envy at the TV cops with their denim shorts.

"Of course, when the time comes," he added, "those guys will have to put on real, uniform, heavy-duty regulation pants and make like *real* officers."

"Yes," said Alison, charging her voice with sympathy. "That should wipe the grins off their faces. . . . Er, when will that be, sir? When will they be doing the final take?"

"Huh, *hours* yet, the way these things go!" growled the policeman. He turned and, raising his voice to a regulation heavy-duty level, addressed the crowd as a whole. "Now come on, folks, keep well back, move it, move it. . . ."

They shuffled back a few steps.

Then:

"Hey!" he barked, glaring in the opposite direction, beyond the knot of television people and past the bushes to someone across the highway. "You! . . . Get back over here behind the cameras. Can't you see that's where the action is?"

Which is when Alison got her big idea.

"Come on," she said softly, plucking at her companions' shirts. "Let's go."

"But I wanna *watch!*" wailed Jeannie.

"Yes," said Emmeline. "We only just got here, Ally. What's the—?"

"Sure! sure!" murmured Alison. "But there are better places than this."

"But—you heard what the policeman *said*. . . ."

"I know. I heard."

Something in her voice made them follow her, back through the tunnel under the highway. A tearing sound above their heads told them that yet another dummy run was taking place in the chase scene.

Suddenly Emmeline stopped.

"Hey, now just a minute, Ally! Don't tell me you're intending to watch it from the opposite side!"

Alison blinked, all brown-eyed innocence.

"Sure. Why not?"

"But you heard what the cop said. We'll be in the way there. In front of the cameras. We might show up in the background of the scene, and they wouldn't want that, and—"

"Come on!" said Alison, plucking her friend's shirt again and giving Jeannie a gently steering shove with the other hand. "There are bushes over here, too. We can hide behind them."

"But won't there be a policeman over on this side?" asked Jeannie, slightly breathless as she began to get the drift of her sister's plans.

"Sure. Two more, in fact. And there they are, see. With nothing to do but keep out of the way themselves."

This was true. All the girls had to do was get down in the long grass at the side of the highway and gradually ease their way to the bushes opposite the ramp. The policemen were looking out for ordinary pedestrians who might come blundering along unwittingly. The possibility of human grass snakes hadn't entered their heads. It was a cinch.

"So now what?" said Emmeline, when they were safely in the bushes. "We could see better over there, and if we stick our heads out they'll see us."

"Yeah!" said Jeannie. "And I'm getting bitten all over by ticks!"

Patiently (for she could be very patient when it really suited her), Alison explained:

"We do not stick our heads out fully until the final take. We keep peeping out carefully until the star himself arrives. Then we'll know it's going to be the final take. Then we do stick our heads out. And the rest of our bodies."

"But—but—" Emmeline was nearly choking with alarm. "But won't it spoil the scene?"

"Spoil it? Hah! It'll *make* it! I mean, what could be more natural than innocent bystanders being startled by the chase? I'm surprised the producer couldn't see that himself, and ask for volunteers from the crowd."

"You mean—?"

"I mean we play the part properly. We rear up and stare in horror. It's our big chance. It's what we used to *pray* for when we were just fooling around on the apartment TV, isn't it?"

"Ooh, yes!" cried Jeannie.

"Be quiet!" growled Alison, pulling her down.

"Sorry!" murmured Jeannie, all won over now, her bites forgotten. "Sorry, Ally! But, gee—you're right. Is *this* a good look of horror?"

It wasn't. But they had nearly an hour to spend in those bushes, practicing, and when the Great Star finally arrived and the TV cops got into their long pants and the cars and cameras went into action, the girls were ready. As the vehicles squealed to a stop, out from the bushes came three faces, contorted with horror, outrage, and naked fear, and up flew six arms in various gestures of amazement and shock.

"Now down again!" commanded Alison. "Quick!"

She had judged that everybody would have been

too busy concentrating on the scene in the foreground to notice their contribution.

"If we don't make ourselves too obvious now, they'll not even know we're in the scene until it's been printed. Then the producer will be only too glad we *did* make our guest appearances. You'll see."

Well, nobody raised a shout. And since the whole group disbanded immediately after that, the girls guessed they had gotten away with it.

"Gosh!" said Emmeline, as they emerged from the bushes a quarter of an hour later, when people had started resuming their normal activities on the highway again. "Us! On television! With *him!*"

"Yeah!" squealed Jeannie, doing a neat forward roll in the grass to express her delight. *"Us! Terrific!"*

Alison was equally excited, equally delighted. But she had decided that it would be more fitting for one of the great careers of all time to begin on a touchingly modest note—something that would look good when they wrote about her in *TV Guide* in years to come.

"Emmeline," she said, placing a gentle hand on her friend's plump forearm, "I shall never forget that you were the cause of this."

"Of—of what, Ally?"

"Of me getting my first big chance."

3

"It's really happening!"

That had all taken place months ago, and in the interval the girls had lost much of their early excitement. But with the news that at last *their* episode was definitely going to be screened, the excitement had all bubbled up again, so that now, when that episode had started to flicker its way across the family screen—across *millions* of family screens—even Alison found it hard not to squirm and wriggle on the couch.

"Where *is* Emmeline?" she muttered, yet again, while the Great Detective went through one of his comic routines with a sergeant at police headquarters.

She risked a glance behind her. She had a shrewd notion that a chase such as the one they'd witnessed would come toward the end of the episode, but she didn't want to take too many chances.

"It would be just like her to get here when it was all over and—"

Alison broke off, not sure whether the buzz she

had heard had come from her own front door or from that of an apartment which had suddenly appeared on the screen: a place where someone was being held captive.

None of the actors turned to *their* door.

"I think this must be Emmeline now," said Mrs. McNair.

Jeannie launched herself off the couch like a small green rocket with a flaming warhead.

"I'll get it! I'll get it!" she squealed.

Then:

"Emmeline, *darling,* my *sweet!*" they heard her say, in raucous imitation of Alison's theatrical manner. "We're on, we're on! Any minute now!"

"Come on in, honey," said Mrs. McNair, looking up. "You haven't missed much."

Alison was too annoyed to turn around.

"Where've you been?" she muttered grumpily, as she felt the bounce of Jeannie and the heavier slump of her friend on the couch beside her.

"I—I'm sorry, Alison."

Something in Emmeline's voice made Alison look at her sharply for a moment. (It was safe. The scene on the screen was still set in that other apartment. Someone was making a ransom demand, with a handkerchief over the telephone mouthpiece.)

Then Alison blinked.

Emmeline's face looked tragic. More tragic even than the Fisherman's Wife expression. There was something blank about it, a stunned look, that was far more impressive than all the lip-chewing and eye-crinkling that Emmeline indulged in in front of the

24

elevator cameras. Moreover, she was not dressed in the way they had agreed and planned to dress. She was still in the old pair of jeans and the faded yellow sweater she'd been wearing earlier.

"You haven't *changed!*" murmured Alison, with a strange mixture of concern, curiosity, annoyance, and disgust. "You said—"

"I know! But—" Now Emmeline *was* chewing her lip, but unconsciously and therefore still very effectively. "I—oh, Ally—something terrible—"

"Shush!"

A squeal of brakes from the screen had claimed Alison's attention, despite her newly aroused curiosity about Emmeline's state of mind.

"I think the chase is starting now."

Emmeline sniffed as if she couldn't have cared less. Jeannie jumped up, standing on the couch and rapidly jouncing up and down. Alison leaned forward, absorbed.

But she'd been premature. This was merely the Great Detective being driven to the scene of a killing.

Jeannie leaned against the back of the couch, still standing, and slowly slid to a sitting position again. As she did so, she came out with one of her rare but blinding flashes of common sense.

"What we have to look for, I guess, is the man in the blazer and straw hat. When *he* comes on—"

"Sure, sure!" snapped Alison. "When he comes on we'll know it's nearly time. I was just going to say that."

Well, be that as it may, the mention of the man in the straw hat had a very strong effect on everyone in the room. Even Mr. and Mrs. McNair and Tom seemed to sit up more alertly after that. Watching out for the beginning of a car chase had really been too vague an undertaking. It could have begun with any old street scene, or it could suddenly have been sprung on them out of the blue. But watching for this single distinctive figure was different. It guaranteed success. It promised to give them not only the action they were waiting for, but also the time to settle down to focus on it properly. It was like watching for the first majorette in a big parade, or the referee climbing into the ring before a big fight, or the conductor stepping onto the podium at a band concert. It was hypnotic.

Even Emmeline fell under its spell, obviously forgetting for the time being whatever burden of trouble she had sunk down on the couch with. Some of the color came back to her cheeks and a faint sparkle to her eyes. And so they all watched, with this new intentness, with a raptness that would have had the scriptwriter and producer glowing with pleasure.

"*That's* the way to get an audience watching a program!" the producer might have said.

"Yeah, right on the edges of their seats!" the scriptwriter would probably have added.

Yet really the plot and the acting and the directing had nothing to do with it. Not one of the six people in that room could have told you, even minutes afterward, exactly what the story was all about. Nobody was the least bit excited by the shooting that broke out from time to time. Nobody was the least bit anxious about the fate of the kidnaped man. Nobody

26

was the least bit impressed by the detective's brilliant deductions or the smart cracks he kept making to his assistants.

All that these viewers were looking out for was the appearance of a large white straw hat. All they were listening for was the mention of such an article.

And the mention came first.

Someone on the screen said that the ransom money would be picked up by a man in a white straw hat and the cops better not follow him or else.

Then there was pandemonium in the McNair apartment.

"This is it!" growled Mr. McNair.

"Oh yes!" cried his wife.

And even Tom was moved to say, in a drawl that failed to mask a quiver of excitement:

"Here we go for the Three Stooges bit, I guess!"

As for the girls, they literally fell about.

Jeannie gave a squeal and decided she'd get a sharper view by crouching over the rug with her back to the television set and looking at the screen upside down between her legs. Emmeline clutched at Alison's waist as if in danger of being swept away by a heavy wave, murmuring, "Oh—oh—I hardly dare look!" And Alison clutched back at Emmeline's shoulders as if in danger of being lifted by a whirlwind and carried up and away and out of range of the set just at the crucial moment.

"He's *there!*" shrieked Jeannie.

"And here's his cab!" cried Tom, no longer even trying to sound cool.

"And there's the unmarked police car," murmured

Alison, feeling sick with suppressed excitement. "Are you watching, su—su—?" She just couldn't say "sweetie" this time. "Em! Em!" she whispered urgently, instead.

"I—I'm watching!" moaned Emmeline. "Oh, it's really happening! The man's pointing a gun at the cab driver! He knows he's being followed!"

"The chase, it seems, is on," said Mr. McNair.

He sounded dry and unconcerned, but his haunches barely touched the edge of his chair.

And so indeed the chase was on, amid a lot of traffic at first, in busy streets. But soon it was as if the cars had been shot free from a whirlpool of other cars, and they were on their own—the yellow one with the green checkers and the brown one with the flashing red light—roaring up what seemed like a suburban lane, past bushes, but which soon turned out to be—

"The ramp!" cried Emmeline. "It's—we—"

But things were happening faster than speech on that screen. Between Emmeline's first two words, the marked police cars suddenly rocketed into the picture. Between her second two words, the first blue-and-white car had squealed to a swerving halt in front of the cab.

Alison thrust her friend aside and moved forward, eyes fixed on the screen like a hunter stalking a nervous and highly elusive animal.

"The background, the background!" she muttered. "Keep watching the background!"

But it was no good.

The background was a greenish-blue blur. And the

camera kept zooming in: on the Great Detective's face, on the guns of the cops, on the despair in the eyes of the straw-hat man. With every change of angle, the background changed too, of course, so that even if it hadn't been blurred and out of focus, it would have been difficult to spot the right stretch of bushes.

"Ouch!"

Jeannie had nearly sprained her neck, trying to follow the switches from her upside-down position.

And then it was over: just as Alison thought she had detected a group of faint pinkish shadows among the greenery, a smudge of reddish gold, a flash of something white. The scene had moved to police headquarters.

Alison saw the whole screen blur up as she turned away and fought, with bitter ferocity, to hide her disappointment.

"But—but it took all *afternoon,* didn't it, Emmeline?" Jeannie was upright now, looking dazed, as the end titles came up on the screen. "I mean—that took only *seconds!*"

"I guess they might have cut some out," murmured Emmeline. She sounded resigned. Already her earlier trouble was returning to her mind, judging from the heavy sigh that followed her words, and the faraway, rather frightened look in her blue eyes.

Tom was smirking.

"Sure they cut something out!" he said. "You don't think they'd leave you three freaks in, do you? They were playing for thrills, not laughs. Now if—"

"That's enough, Tom!" his father said.

"It must have been very interesting, watching them

shoot that," said Mrs. McNair, giving her daughters (and particularly the elder one) an anxious sidelong glance.

But Alison was not to be consoled. Her eyes were dry—having been surreptitiously wiped on the corner of the back of the couch—but they were blazing now: a pair of extra, larger, crowning sequins.

She stood up and walked jerkily to the door, every muscle in her legs and arms tensed up in her fight to appear casual and unconcerned.

"Come on!" she said to the others—and nearly choked on the second word. "On!" she repeated, just to show she *had* control of her voice. "Come—*on!*"

They didn't really need telling twice.

Jeannie was feeling as if she'd done something to be ashamed of and was in a hurry to hide her face. Emmeline had worries of her own and was urgently needing to share them with her best friend.

"Alison," she said, as soon as they were out in the corridor, "I have to tell you *why* I was late. It—"

"Oh, what does it matter?" said Alison, with a fiery toss of her hair. "You could have missed the whole program and it wouldn't have mattered."

"Yes, but—"

"Oh, be quiet!"

It was a rude thing to say. But as she flung open the door of her room, Alison knew it wasn't half as bad as what she felt like saying, which was:

"Emmeline, I shall never forgive you for being the cause of this!"

And it was a good thing she did hold back those words, too. Apart from being cruel and unfair and a

30

mockery of what she'd said before, on the way back from the West Side Highway, they would probably have caused Emmeline to break down completely and run off home in tears.

Then they might never have heard about her trouble until it was far too late to do anything about it.

4
Alison's Fury

"Who told *you* to come in here with us? Oh, stay if you want!"

That—all in the same breath—was addressed to Jeannie, as Alison stormed with flashing eyes and flashing limbs into the room.

"And *you*—get off the bed!"

That—in the very next breath—was addressed to Norton, the blue-gray cat, who was sitting Sphinx-like, with slitted green eyes, on Alison's pillow.

He didn't move. Those eyes had a knowing, sly, slightly amused expression. He seemed to be saying he could have told them they would be wasting their time, looking for themselves in that flickering box in the other room. And his unruffled immobility actually did say that furthermore he wasn't fooled by Alison's tone. His whole comfortable, furry body proclaimed with a deeply purring persistence that Alison's anger was as harmless as it was random and restless. It was quick and bright but not vicious, as it went playing over everything she happened to glance upon, casting a glare on it, then moving on. Mere summer lightning. Norton dipped his head and closed his eyes.

Yet she *was* furious.

Although what she had thought of as her "guest appearance" had been kept a secret from Tom, she had gone to great lengths to alert everyone at school. They would all have been watching—teachers as well as students. Some of them would have been writhing with envy, sure, but they wouldn't have been able to keep their eyes off that program.

And she had confidently expected a flood of calls and visits after the show, from friends and rivals alike. Including even Greg Peters, the handsome senior who lived in the same building but never gave her more than a brief passing glance, as a rule. Even he would have had to pay proper attention to her now she was a star, and she had imagined him appearing shyly, rather shamefaced, at the back of the crowd outside the apartment door, fumbling with a bunch of flowers he'd hurriedly snatched from one of his mother's vases. Wasn't that why she'd taken such extra special care over her preparations?

Suddenly her fury became concentrated.

Her glance had fallen on the poster, tacked to the wall: the huge magnified head of the Great Detective himself, seeming to jeer at her the way he jeered at his assistants.

"You're a *rotten* detective anyway!" she yelled, tearing it down with a ripping noise that accompanied the word "rotten" and sent Norton leaping off and under the bed, ears flat.

"Now *that,*" the quivering tip of his disappearing tail seemed to say, "that *was* lightning!"

Jeannie was staring at the shredded star, one strip of his face still hanging on the wall, the rest in a crumpled ball on the bed, just where the cat had been.

"But you always said he was the best, Alison," she murmured cautiously, yet with a gleam in her eye that betrayed a hope to witness more destruction, so long as the lightning didn't strike *her*.

"I know what I said!" snarled Alison. "The best of a lousy bunch is what I meant." She snatched at the remaining strip, crumpled it, and flung it across the room, just grazing the head of the doleful Emmeline, who was sitting slumped on a chair. Her friend didn't flinch, didn't even seem to have noticed the missile. "He's nothing but a—a—" The image of that close-up switch to the detective's face flashed back in Alison's mind: the switch that had blotted out the much more interesting background. "A great fat camera-hog!"

Then her anger shied from the actor back to the part he played.

"Detective? Hyah! Overrated! *Dumb* really! I could do just as well myself. You bet. Think I couldn't?"

No one challenged those flashing eyes, not even Norton, who knew everything, but now stayed under the bed.

"Sure I could! If *I'd* got the whole of the New York Police Department behind me."

"Oh, Ally!" said Emmeline, as Alison was getting her breath back. "That's just what—"

"It's true!" said Alison, turning on her friend as if ready to blast her down the middle, too, and crumple half of her into a ball to be flung across the room. "If only I had a crime to investigate, I'd show you. Even without the N.Y.P.D. behind me."

Emmeline shrugged. Sometimes it was just too much, trying to keep up with her friend's changes of direction. There Ally had been, storming mad because an actor's face had blotted her out of the background (as if the poor man could be blamed for that!)—and now it was the *character* he'd been playing that she was criticizing.

Jeannie was more sympathetic. She liked the way Alison was beginning to veer. The younger girl couldn't have expressed it in words but, knowing her sister, she could sense that this new direction had great possibilities.

She also knew how to keep her sister going in any given direction. Jeannie was a good lightning-conductor where her sister was concerned.

She pretended to be doubtful.

"Well, there's plenty of crime out there," she said, waving toward the window and the rumble of city traffic.

"Yes," said Emmeline, taking heart again. "In fact—"

"We've been through this before," said Alison. "And the crimes out there are either too big, like armed robbery, or too petty"—here she glared at

36

Jeannie—"like who put a frog in your lunch box at school."

"Well, I didn't think it was pretty, when I opened the box and its big, bulgy eyes stared up at me, and—"

"*Petty,* I said. Not *pretty.* Trivial. Futile. Peanuts. Penny-ante. . . . Oh, be quiet or you leave this room!"

"Well, the picture-stealing wasn't peanuts!" said Jeannie hotly. "And we solved that!"

"*Solved* nothing!" snapped Alison. "We just stumbled into it, that's all. True, I had to act with great courage." Her voice became less argumentative here, her eyes dreamy. "And because of that courage the thieves were apprehended." For a few moments she was back in her witchcraft mood, remembering the time when she thought she'd been under Magical Attack from a witch in a house opposite.* As it happened, the woman had merely been spying out for an accomplice. So it was quite true that by launching a Magical Counter-Attack and uncovering the crime in the process, Alison had "stumbled" into it. "Yes," she murmured, "I might have been killed. . . ."

The other two girls looked at each other. Alison seemed to be going into a trance. Was she thinking of taking up witchcraft again?

There were still a few dusty relics of her witching days scattered about the room: a length of steel chain looped over the door; a huge padlock hanging from an iron hook over the window; the corner of

* For a full account, see *The Active-Enzyme Lemon-Freshened Junior High School Witch.*

her Magical Workbook sticking out from a pile of magazines at the side of the bed.

But no. Alison's eyes snapped open.

"What I'd like," she said crisply, angrily, back in the smarting present again, "is something closely connected with our own lives—"

"Well, the frog—"

"But a *real* crime, something needing careful investigation, the sort of thing that *that* big dummy would be asked to investigate." She swept the crumpled half of "that big dummy's" face from the bed and sat down. Her eyes were gleaming now rather than flashing, and they were quite still. "Something needing real scientific methods, some really *new,* really modern crime. Something really—"

"And that's what I keep trying to tell you!" cried Emmeline, getting up and coming across to stand over her friend. "That's why I was *late!*"

Something in her voice arrested Alison. She looked up sharply.

"Huh?"

"Yes!" said Emmeline. "Because a crime like that —exactly like that—has just happened to—to my father—and—and—oh, Ally! oh, Jeannie!—it's su-su-*serious!*"

And then at last she did burst into tears.

5
The Crime

Alison waited with tightly stretched patience for Emmeline to finish sobbing.

Jeannie, who couldn't bear to see anyone crying without doing something to help, had immediately flung her arms around Emmeline's shaking shoulders and started hugging her. This of course only prolonged the bout. As Jeannie squeezed, out gushed more tears. It reminded Alison of a pump—and this particular well seemed bottomless.

"That's enough," she said gently, but with a very firm tug at her sister's collar. "Here, Emmeline"— she thrust out a bunch of tissues—"dry your face and tell us about this crime."

Emmeline gulped, then started dabbing.

"Well . . . as you know . . . Daddy works for a credit-card company . . . here in town . . . Newcharge Incorporated."

"Yes—so?"

"So—so that's what it's all about. He's gone and lost his *own* Newcharge card . . . oh, gosh!"

For an instant it looked as if Emmeline might break down again. Alison put another firm grip on Jeannie's collar and steered her out of reach of Emmeline.

"But that's not a crime," she said.

Emmeline sniffed.

"It is in the eyes of his boss."

"Yes, but you said a *real* crime!" Alison was beginning to sound very impatient now. "Something for us to investigate. Something the police might be given to investigate."

Emmeline sighed. Then bit her lip as it started to quiver.

"Yes, well . . . losing his card was just the—the start of it. . . ."

"Don't cry, Em!"

"Shut up, Jeannie, for heaven's sakes! That's all she needs to set her off again. . . . Pull yourself together, Emmeline Grant! We can't help you if we don't know the facts. O.K.?"

"O . . . O.K. . . ." Emmeline took a huge sniff inside the limp wad of tissues. "Well—it happened on Monday, and—"

"But that was four days ago. You said—"

"Jeannie, if you don't be quiet you go out! Let Emmeline tell it her own way."

"Yes, well . . ."

Then Emmeline did tell it her own way. Her account was punctuated by sniffs and snivels at first, but gradually, as she realized she had Alison's full and fiercely focused attention, her voice grew more confident and her words more fluent.

Monday had been Mrs. Grant's birthday. That afternoon, on his way home from work, Mr. Grant had stopped by at the florist's on the corner of Madison Avenue near their apartment. There he bought for his wife a big bunch of red carnations, using his Newcharge card.

"They were beautiful!" Here Emmeline nearly broke down again. Then she caught a glimpse of Alison's expression and bit her lip hard. She went on: "Well, he was in a rush. He had to get ready for the party and he was late already. So when he noticed someone he didn't want to stop to talk with—someone who was waiting to cross at the traffic lights just opposite the store—"

"Just a second. He was still in the store?"

"Yes, looking out of the window, while the store lady was charging the flowers to his card. Why?"

"No. I was just thinking that's maybe where he left it. At the florist's. Being in such a hurry and all."

"No, worse luck! He got the card back all right, but instead of replacing it carefully in his wallet, he shoved it into his raincoat pocket and hurried out."

"Ah!" said Alison.

"Yeah, ah!" murmured Emmeline morosely. "Because that's the last he saw of it."

"You should never stuff things like money into your raincoat pock—"

"Jeannie!"

"Sorry, Ally. But—"

"Go on, Emmeline. When did he discover it was missing?"

"Oh, fairly soon! He remembered it when he was

getting changed for the party. And always being very careful about his credit cards—well . . . *nearly* always . . ."

"Sure!" muttered Alison. "Sure! . . . So?"

"So he went straight to his raincoat to transfer his card but—no card. Not in any of the pockets."

"My new raincoat's got a secret pocket with a button to keep it closed and—"

"I wish your mouth had! Be quiet!"

Jeannie went through the motions of buttoning her lip, under Alison's glare.

"So go on, Emmeline. I guess he searched everywhere?"

"You bet! He was an hour late for the party, but it couldn't be helped. He searched the apartment, the elevator, the lobby—even the street between the building and the corner, where the store is. Even the store itself, between the counter and the door. But—still no card."

"But maybe someone picked it up! Didn't he think of *that?*" said Jeannie.

She looked from face to face, wide-eyed in her triumph.

"Of course he did, stupid!" said Alison. "Uh—I guess."

She looked inquiringly at Emmeline.

"Oh sure!" said Emmeline. "He could hardly think of anything else. But at first he *hoped*. He hoped that that 'someone' was honest. That they'd mail it right back to the company. So every morning this week he's gone to the office specially early to go through the mail first. But it hasn't turned up."

"Well, so what?" said Alison, as patiently as she could, seeing signs of a fresh flood of tears. "There's time yet. And anyway"—her voice hardened—"it's really only a lost card. It still isn't a *real* crime, whatever your father's boss thinks."

"Yes, but—but I haven't finished! Today—oh dear—"

Emmeline fought bravely to bring her mouth under control. The others waited in silence, Jeannie looking ready to burst into tears herself at the drop of a single one of Emmeline's, and Alison with tightly crossed fingers and even tighter lips. Then Emmeline continued:

"All—all purchases made with Newcharge cards are recorded. You know—they come through on a computer or something. There's always a day or two's gap. But—well—today, the computer came up with four new charges on Daddy's card. All four made *after* the flowers he'd used it for on Monday. The first charge was made on Tuesday. Then Wednesday, yesterday, three. Three more items, all in one day."

"Somebody's *using* it!" cried Jeannie.

This time Alison ignored the interruption. Her eyes were glowing.

"So it *is* a real crime," she murmured. Then, remembering she was talking to the distressed daughter of the victim, she said more sympathetically: "But can't the card be stopped? Isn't that what happens when a credit card is lost or stolen and the company is notified? So that the owner of the card doesn't have to pay?"

Emmeline nodded sadly.

"It has. It has been stopped. In a way, that's all been taken care of. It was put on the stolen list today. But that won't reach all the stores for another week. And in the meantime the stores aren't likely to run a telephone check with the company for any purchase under one hundred dollars." Emmeline was speaking in a dull monotone, as if she knew all this by heart, having heard her father go over it time and time again in his anxiety. "So you see, Ally—if the thief keeps to articles under one hundred dollars, which he seems to be doing—he must be very smart —why, he can go on for days yet, buying all sorts of items."

Alison nodded, frowning.

"And that mounts up, right?" she said.

"Your father could lose *thousands* of dollars!" blurted Jeannie.

Emmeline shook her head.

"No, honey. It won't be *his* money that's lost. *He* won't have to pay, now that the card has been put on the list. It'll be the company's loss."

"Oh well, that's all right then," said Jeannie.

"It is *not* all right!" said Emmeline wearily. "I keep telling you. He's likely to lose more than money because of this. He's—he's likely to lose his *job*."

"Why?" asked Jeannie, looking puzzled.

"Because the president of the company gets really mad even when a *customer* loses his card and costs the company money. And when he gets to hear that one of his own executives has done it, he'll go crazy. Luckily he's in San Francisco at the moment. But when he gets back at the end of next week he's bound to find out. And—oh dear—if the card isn't traced and recovered by then, Daddy will get fired for sure. And—and we'll have to leave the apartment, and maybe go back to Cleveland!"

Alison looked up sharply.

"Why Cleveland?"

Emmeline had started to cry again. It was a steady weeping rather than a jerky sobbing, but somehow it was all the more upsetting to see. There was real misery on the plump girl's wet face as she turned it to Alison.

"Because that's where the family business is. Selling wood and nails and things to carpenters and builders. And if he can't get another job in New York, that's what he'll have to do. Go back there and—oh, Ally! *Can* you help to find the thief? I mean *really?*"

Alison thought of Mr. Grant: a pleasant, mild-mannered little man, not a lot taller than his daughter. He wasn't much to look at, even as fathers go, but he always spoke to the girls as if they were grown up, deserving respect, and not just targets for weak jokes.

She also thought of Mrs. Grant: another small person, who had a loud laugh and a brisk manner, as if to make up for her husband's mildness. But she was very kind, and she always treated Alison as if the girl was a good influence on her daughter. That again was very unusual where parents were concerned, thought Alison, remembering her own mother's sometimes cutting remarks about Emmeline.

But most of all, in that three- or four-second spell that seemed to last for minutes, Alison thought about Emmeline herself, and all the good times they'd had together and the troubles they'd shared. Em could be a bit trying at times, a bit too ready to burst into tears, like now. But even when she was scared or timid about something, she never deserted Alison—which made her all the better friend, when you came to think of it.

"*Sure* we'll help you, Em!" she said softly, putting a hand on her friend's shoulder.

Two of the fingers of that hand were crossed. This was because at that moment Alison wanted nothing more than to get Mr. Grant out of trouble and ensure that the family stayed right where they were.

Then she remembered the other, more selfish aspects of the case. How she'd been burning to make up for the humiliation of that non-appearance on TV. How she'd cried out for a chance to solve a real crime. How she'd boasted how much better she'd be than the Great Detective himself.

Well, there was no going back on that boast now. As well as Mr. Grant's job, there was her own *face* to save.

So she became more like her usual self.

Taking her hand off Emmeline's shoulder, she reached over to the pile of magazines and plucked out the Magical Workbook.

"Remember this?" she said, flicking over the pages to the last entry.

It concerned their tangle with the art thieves, and their meeting with a real policewoman—one who had red hair like her own—and how Alison had resolved there and then to switch from witching to detecting —to becoming, in fact:

a Lady Detective like Angie Morrison, though even better because I shall start in right away (with Emmeline as my rather dumb but trustworthy assistant) by being a GIRL detective—a Top-flight Fully-automated Junior High School Girl Detective.

Well, things hadn't worked out like that at first— there being no suitable crimes to solve, nothing worthy of her talents—and she had let her resolution lapse and gather dust like the Workbook itself.

But now—she blew the dust from the book in a cloud that caused the emerging Norton to sneeze and dive back under the bed—now she had something to get her teeth into.

"Right!" she said, snapping the book shut and looking at her assistants. "Here's what we do. We plan our investigations tonight and we start right in with the legwork tomorrow morning, first thing."

6
Legwork

Friday turned out to be a clear crisp day—perfect for the "legwork" Alison had mentioned. As it happened, though, they never had to walk more than a few hundred feet throughout the whole of that first day of their investigations.

"Our first move," Alison had said, the night before, "is to make a systematic search along the route. Where the card *must* have been dropped. Between the florist's and your apartment, Emmeline."

"Well, at least it isn't far," Emmeline had said dubiously, not seeing much point in this. "Less than a block, really."

Jeannie had been more outspoken.

"Search? But it was four days ago! And anyway—we *know* the card's been picked up already, don't we?"

"I'm not talking about a search for the card itself, stupid! I mean a search for anyone who was around at the time. Eyewitnesses. People who might have seen someone picking the card up, and can give us a description, something to work on."

Emmeline had brightened a little at that. It sounded a *bit* positive, and she was yearning for action. Even so, she'd continued to look doubtful.

"I guess that means waiting around until five in the afternoon, then."

Alison had decided her friend needed jollying along. She patted the plump shoulder.

"Smart figuring, Sergeant!"

A flash of jealousy had crossed Jeannie's eyes.

"What's smart about *that?*"

"Because that was the time of day, more or less." Emmeline's patient voice had smoothed Jeannie's ruffled feelings almost immediately, in the way that made Jeannie sometimes wish Emmeline were her sister and Alison just a friend. "That was when Daddy lost the card, around five, five-thirty. And the same people are likely to be around at that time, coming home from work. It—"

"Even smarter figuring, though," Alison had interrupted, tearing off a blank leaf from the Magical Workbook, "is to get busy right away, first thing in the morning, on the sort of people who're around *all day*. Then we needn't waste time waiting until late afternoon. *People like*"—here she'd raised her voice to check Jeannie's question—"people like"—she was scribbling away—"these . . ."

Then she'd presented them with her first list, or, as she'd headed it:

TASK SHEET ⚹1

Under which she had scrawled:

> *To interview the following:*
> ⚹*Emmeline's building's doorman (the*

one on duty at the time of felony, Mon-
day).

✻ *Other doormen along street.*

✻ *Loafers, kids, cops, etc. (Like who're*
usually hanging around.)

✻ *Women at florist's.*

"You're very thorough, Ally," Emmeline had said,
in a rather awed but much heartened voice.

"In this game you gotta be, baby!" Alison had
replied, already beginning to sound like the Great
Detective himself.

"What's a felony?" was all that Jeannie could
think of saying.

They'd gone on to spend the last ten minutes of
the Thursday night briefing explaining this to the
kid: Alison with overwhelming scorn, Emmeline with
infinite patience.

Since Friday had started out so clear and springlike
—a morning to put you in mind of flowers—and
since Bert (the man who'd been on the door of the
Grants' building on Monday afternoon) wouldn't be
on duty until 1:00 P.M.—and since the florist's was
the last place the card had been seen anyway—that's
where they decided to start.

"One good thing," murmured Alison, as they hurried along there, shortly after nine.

The girls were wearing their most businesslike casual clothes: Alison a brown pants suit; Emmeline a
pair of dark blue slacks and a hip-length belted imitation leather jacket, also dark blue; and Jeannie a
pair of new jeans with a roll-neck, dark green,
chunky-knit sweater.

(Alison had insisted on this type of apparel with far greater force than any school principals ever insisted on *their* dress code. "No frills, no thongs, no fringes, no decorations, O.K.? And nothing disreputable, either, you hear me? Real detective-type clothes. Respectable, for interviewing people in, got it? But *easy,* just in case one of the people being interviewed should prove to be the card thief, and get scared by one of my penetrating questions, and make a break for it, and have to be chased through busy streets, alleyways, maybe over walls, *rooftops* even." Then, caught up in her own imaginings, Alison had also stipulated purses with shoulder straps. "These not only look businesslike, *detectivelike,* but if we fill them with heavy objects they could make very useful weapons. You know, like to hurl at the fugitive's feet, like slings, to trip him with. Or to threaten to zonk him with if we corner him and he turns mean and savage.")

So, that morning, Alison's left shoulder was sagging with the weight of the travel iron in her purse, and Emmeline's with the five-pound box of long-grained rice in hers. Jeannie's only shoulder-strap purse flaunted Disneyland decorations and therefore had the least businesslike look. But she was packing the most sinister weight: a heavy old broken alarm clock that was mostly silent but which occasionally broke out in a loud, bomblike ticking.

"What's a good thing, Ally?" asked Emmeline, when it looked as if her friend was too deep in thought to explain without being prompted.

"Huh?"

"You said just now, 'One good thing.'"

"Oh. Yes. I mean the fact that school's out a whole week before Easter, this year."

"So what's good about that?"

"Well, didn't you say your father's boss—whosis—"

"J. Hickory Haverstashe," said Emmeline, unable to suppress a tremor of apprehension around her mouth and under her eyes. Always uttered in full, like that, it was a name to be feared in her family, now more than ever.

"Yeah. Him," said Alison, with (to Emmeline) shocking irreverence. "Didn't you say he doesn't get back until the end of next week?"

"Yes—oh—you mean—?"

"I mean we'll be free to concentrate on this case until we bust it. *Really* concentrate. All day, every day. A whole week."

Alison was talking as if they'd got forever. Emmeline wasn't anything like so sure. She just sighed.

Jeannie was cheerful, though.

"There's another good thing why there won't be any school for a long time, too."

Alison ignored her kid sister's babble. Emmeline, more polite, said:

"Oh, honey?"

"Yeah! We won't get laughed at and kidded about not being on TV last night. We—"

"Won't we?" muttered Alison grimly.

They had just reached the corner of Madison. A girl coming around it had almost bumped into them. What with the sight of this girl, and the look on her face, and Jeannie's reminder, all plans for the first interview at the florist's were driven from Alison's mind.

52

"Why, *Alison!* Emmeline! And little Junie! What-ever *happened* last night?"

It was Nan Stafford. Nan Stafford, about whom Alison liked not one single thing. Nan Stafford, with the phony British accent she still clung to after spending her last summer vacation in England. Nan Stafford, with the beautiful blue eyes (but cold, and without depth) and fairly good slim figure (but thickish ankles). Nan Stafford, with the unusual light-gold shade of hair (when she washed it), which unfortunately tended to look mousy as a rule. Nan Stafford, who, by some trickery, maybe even black-mail, had managed to become the steady girl friend of poor Greg Peters. Nan Stafford the Creep.

"The name's Jeannie!" said the younger McNair girl, looking almost as fierce as her sister. "And I'm four feet three and three eighths, which is not little!"

"How sweet!" said Nan, making as if to pat Jean-nie on the head, then hurriedly withdrawing her hand as Jeannie made as if to bite it. "But Alison, Emme-line—what *happened?* I watched and watched that program all the way through but didn't catch a glimpse of you. It's true that Greg was with me at the time and my eyes weren't on the screen every sin-gle second. But surely we'd have seen *something* of you if you'd been featured the way you said you were?"

Alison breathed deeply, fingering her purse. Nan Stafford didn't know how near she was just then to feeling the weight of that travel iron.

"It was a—I mean—something went—" Emmeline began stammering.

"There was a technical problem," said Alison, re-

covering her cool. "The star felt we might steal the scene, so they had to do a little cutting."

Well, it was the truth as she'd figured it. And it still left room for the producer to want to know who those kids *were,* particularly that older, red-headed girl, *wow!*

She even managed a smile now.

"So you see, Nan, we haven't heard the last of it yet. They're probably looking over that cut section right now, wondering just what kind of show would really suit our style. But if you'll excuse us, we have some important business to attend to."

"Oh yeah?" murmured Nan Stafford, in a very un-British tone. "Well, if you think you can fool me with all that—"

But the old-fashioned bell on the florist's door drowned out her last words, as Alison—all detective again, and with no time for childish talk—steered her crew into the store and marched purposefully up to the counter.

7

Organized Crime?

The women in the florist's weren't much help. At least not directly.

They were sympathetic enough, when they heard the purpose of the girls' visit. And sure, they remembered Mr. Grant's own visit on Monday.

"Specially as he came in here again the very same evening," said one of the women.

"Asking what you're asking," said the other.

"But we weren't able to help then," said the first woman.

"And we're not able to help now," said the second.

"Though we'd like to," said the first.

"Such a nice man," said the second.

"And a very good customer," said the first.

Alison frowned. Emmeline sighed. Jeannie ticked —or at least the clock in her purse did, breaking the silence into small equal pieces.

She gave it a shake and it stopped.

"So you can't remember anybody—anyone at all— picking something up off your floor Monday evening?"

"That's what we said, honey," said the first woman, turning from a puzzled stare at Jeannie's purse.

"We don't think there was anything there to pick up anyway," said the second. "He must have dropped it outside someplace."

"That wouldn't be a tape recorder she has in there, would it?" said the first woman, turning back to stare at Jeannie's purse. "Because if he—or you—suspect anyone *here* picked up his card—"

Her voice and expression had hardened.

"Oh, gosh, no!" said Emmeline. "It never even entered our heads."

"I'm asking *her,*" said the woman, nodding toward Alison.

"No, absolutely not," said Alison, secretly pleased that she'd been recognized as the tough one. "And that's an alarm clock, not a tape recorder. Show the lady, Jeannie. . . ." When Jeannie had done this, Alison continued—her own expression hardening, "Why do you ask, ma'am? What made you think we'd suspect *you?*"

"Oh, nothing really," said the woman, looking rather embarrassed. "I mean—"

"The fact is," said her companion, "that in some stores and restaurants—big ones, where they have lots of temporary help—certain employees are always on the lookout for misplaced or forgotten credit cards."

"Really?" said Alison, genuinely interested.

"Yes," said the first woman. "But not in small family businesses like this, you understand."

"I did say places where they had lots of transients

working for them," the other woman reminded her. She turned to the girls. "There's quite a big black market for stolen credit cards."

"A regular racket," said her partner.

"Oh dear!" groaned Emmeline. "It's getting to look worse and worse."

"Your father shouldn't worry, though. The credit-card company will stand the loss."

"That's just the trouble!" moaned Emmeline.

But Alison was already steering her out, after thanking the women for their trouble.

She herself was beginning to look quite pleased, as she stood on the sidewalk scribbling in her notebook. True, they had gained no positive information. But what they *had* heard seemed to have lifted the investigation right up into the Big Time category. It—

Well, here is her entry:

> *Interview #1*
> *Florist's, corner of Madison*
> *Direct clues: zilch.*
> *But suggestion we may be on brink*
> *of vast city-wide racket!*

Sadly, the high standard of interviewing began to drop after that. Quite sharply too. Their next inquiry took place outside the front door of the first apartment building on the street, just around the corner from the florist's.

The girls entered into that second interview with high hopes. This was because it was such a logical place for a hastily stowed credit card to have slipped out of someone's raincoat pocket.

"I mean it must have been just trembling on the

edge," Alison explained. "Half in, half out. He can't have gone many steps before it fell."

"That's if it wasn't well inside and didn't fall out until he pulled out his handkerchief or something," said Emmeline, with too much at stake to be eagerly optimistic.

But Alison was already tackling the doorman at the apartment building there.

"Hi!" she said. "Would you happen to have been on duty here, Monday afternoon?"

"Yeah. What of it?"

The man was tall and thin, with a lined, yellowish face. He was chewing some kind of stomach tablets —one after the other, feeding them into his mouth like coins into a slot machine, and dropping the wrappers onto the sidewalk at his feet.

"Keep New York tidy!" said Jeannie, cheerfully picking them up for him. It had been a recent class project at her school, and she'd been taught to do this with a friendly smile and a polite word. *"Please!"*

Alison felt like slapping her, but it was already too late.

The doorman looked as if he felt like *kicking* Jeannie.

"If you had *my* stomach," he growled, "you'd have more important things to worry about! . . . What was your question?" he asked Alison, in the same snappish voice.

"Sorry about that," she said. "But were you on duty around five on Monday afternoon, sir?"

"I said so, didn't I? Afternoon's afternoon, isn't it? After twelve, after *noon*."

"Yes. Sure. Of course. Sorry. Well . . . do you remember seeing anyone picking anything up off the sidewalk around that time?"

Even as she said it, Alison realized how unfortunate the question was in the context—right after Jeannie's dumb rebuke about littering the sidewalk.

"You getting cute or what?" he yelled. "You kids think you can teach your elders how to behave now, that it? Seeing how you all behave so good yourselves, these days, huh? Think a guy has nothing better to do, guy old enough to be your grandfather, been through two wars, fighting to make sure ya *got* a sidewalk to pick up litter off—think a guy like that's got nothing better to do than take cracks from snot-nose kids, huh? Kids that don't even live in the building he works all day outside protecting them from the animals in *this* jungle? Kids that . . ."

And so on, and on, and on, getting into and out of amazing tangles of words, his sentences like rolls of barbed wire.

Alison listened politely, then thanked him when it seemed as if he was through. He would probably have started unwinding a second reel, so warmed up to the subject was he getting, with white froth from the mints bubbling at his mouth corners, but just then a cab arrived with one of the tenants and he went to open the door.

So she took the opportunity to walk away and find a corner at the side of a stoop to write her notes.

"What does that mean?" Jeannie asked, peering over Alison's wrist at the page.

Alison had written:

Interview ✄2
  Doorman: first building on street.
  Was on duty Monday, time of felony.
  Says [crossed out] *Implies he saw*
  nothing being picked up.

Then, heavily underlined, came the words:

  Methinks he doth protest too much?

It was at this last sentence that Jeannie was pointing.

"It looks like your witchy language again, Ally."

Alison gave her a tight-lipped smile.

"It's Shakespeare. You say it when you think someone is getting all mad about something just to cover up. To hide the real truth."

Emmeline gasped.

"You mean you suspect *him,* Alison? You think *he* might have picked up Daddy's card? You think he's got an uneasy conscience?"

"Well—" Alison frowned. She remembered she hadn't actually mentioned a credit card. Maybe it was simply an uneasy stomach that had caused the outburst, after all. "You never know. You can't afford to rule out anything or anyone when you're dealing with organized crime."

8

The Informant

It was a bad morning for doorman interviews. There were three other apartment buildings in the block, between that first one and Emmeline's, but not one of the three men there had been on duty on Monday afternoon.

"So I guess we'll just have to leave it until after lunch," said Emmeline, with a sigh.

"Huh?"

Alison was staring back along the street.

"I said—"

"Now *here's* someone who might be able to help," said Alison. "Come on."

At first the other two didn't know who she meant. They looked at each other inquiringly as they followed her. Jeannie shrugged. Then Emmeline's face cleared.

"Oh yes! Of course!"

Alison was approaching the large, shabby, shapeless, stooping figure of a man. His hair was gray. He wore a gray checkered shirt. His pants were gray— creased and stained and voluminous—bagging around

his knees, but tucked into gray-white socks at the bottom. His shoes might have started out brown or black, but they too were gray now. Even the much-creased skin at the back of his neck and forearms and elbows seemed gray—or at least a grayish-brown.

"Mr. O'Connor?"

Alison tapped him lightly on one of those wrinkled elbows. He was busy poking into a trash basket with the short polished wooden stick he always used for the purpose. He had once told Emmeline that he'd been a sergeant-major in the Royal Irish Guards over in Britain and that this had been what he called his "swagger stick." Emmeline believed him, but Alison had always had doubts.

"I don't think he's ever been *near* Ireland," she'd said. "I wouldn't mind betting he's been poking around in New York trash baskets ever since he left school. Not that I hold it against him. He's kind of nice."

He turned around sharply now with what could hardly have been called a nice look in his eyes. But when he saw who it was, his expression softened.

"Ah, Kathleen, me girl!" he said. (He always called Alison that, and she'd long since given up trying to correct him.) "A good morning to ya. And you too, Janet, me sweet. And Adeline."

Both "Janet" and "Adeline" opened their mouths in protest, not having given up hope themselves, but "Kathleen" frowned them quiet.

"Mr. O'Connor," she said, "we have a problem."

The man had resumed his prodding. He turned up

a cigarette pack, tapping it expertly to see if it was really empty.

"Then let's be hearing it," he murmured. "And call me Kevin."

"Well, Mr.—er—Kevin . . . Emmeline's father lost something the other afternoon, Monday, in this street, and we were wondering—"

"If you could tell me the nature of the article I might be able to help you. It wouldn't have been a yellow necktie, would it, Adeline? With little red horseshoes on it?"

Emmeline shook her head.

"Nothing like that, I'm afraid."

"Oh!" Mr. O'Connor sniffed wheezily and gave his pants a hitch. From their depths came an odd rustling and clinking, as if the many folds concealed huge pockets, three feet deep and filled with the day's finds. "Well that's a pity, because it was Monday afternoon I found just such an article, not far from this very exact spot I'm standing on. . . . What was it then?" he said, turning to Alison with a new crispness of tone and shrewdness of eye. "Something more valuable?"

"A credit card," said Alison. "And—"

"Pah! A credit card!" Mr. O'Connor swung around to the basket. It looked as if he was going to spit in it, but he gave its contents an angry stirring with the stick instead. "Don't talk to me about them things!"

"Oh?" said Alison, raising her eyebrows. "And why not?"

"Because they're bad for business, that's why! Ruination!"

65

Emmeline's eyes widened.

"Oh, but Daddy says they're just the opposite! They encourage people to spend more and—"

"*My* business, I mean," said Mr. O'Connor, giving the trash a last vicious jab before turning and blinking at the girls. He still looked annoyed, but he was obviously not blaming *them*. He even managed a wry smile. "Listen, darlings," he said. "There was a time, before credit cards became the rage, when a guy could be sure of picking up a dollar's worth of loose change every five blocks, per day. Sometimes more. Now I'm lucky if I find as much as a quarter, same area, same time. It's wicked the difference it's made."

"You mean money that people drop out of their purses and pockets?" said Jeannie.

"Yeah."

"But don't you ever find credit cards?" asked Alison.

Mr. O'Connor blinked, looked down at his stick, inspected it, closed one eye, and took sight along the stick, down to the scuffed gray tip of his left shoe.

"Well—no—I mean not often—I mean maybe oncet —just the one time."

"When? When?" asked Alison and Emmeline almost together.

He looked up, alarmed.

"Oh, not recent! No. No . . . About a year ago is when I'm talking about. Yeah. All of that."

The girls looked disappointed. Alison was the first to rally, as a new idea took shape.

"What did you do with it, Mr.—uh—Kevin?"

He frowned.

"Turned it in, a-course!"

"Was there a reward?"

"Nargh!"

"Well—" Alison fumbled in her purse. She was taking a risk of offending the man, she knew. But it couldn't be helped. "Here," she said, handing him a quarter.

His grimy hand reached out and closed over the coin automatically. Then the fingers uncurled slowly and he hesitated over what to do with it next.

"Say—"

"Go on. Take it. It's yours."

His eyes narrowed.

"Was it somebody you know, Kathleen? Because, believe me, a quarter ain't anything like the value of—"

"No! Don't get me wrong. That's for information. . . . There could be more."

"Yeah?"

The gray-brown face brightened. The fingers closed and the hand went back to one of his pockets. Alison quipped afterward that she counted to three before she heard the coin reach the bottom. But just now she was deadly serious.

"Yes," she said. "We're looking for information about a credit card that was lost recently."

"Monday, you mean?" he asked sharply. Then he scratched his head. "Well, gee, I honestly don't recall finding *any* credit card, save the one I just told you about."

"No," said Alison. "But tell us this. What happens if someone dishonest finds one?" She glanced at Mr.

O'Connor's shabby clothes and, as tactfully as she knew how, added: "I mean someone dishonest but also—well—you know—who maybe isn't dressed well enough to go into a store and use it himself?"

He gave the wry smile again. His eyes twinkled like a pair of dropped brand-new nickels lying in a dusty gutter.

"Like maybe somebody in *these* duds, huh?" he said. "No, don't apologize. You got a point. Your old friend Kevin wouldn't get away with it even if he was dishonest enough to try . . . which he ain't!" he growled. "But, you know, there *is* channels," he went on. "I mean it's only what I heard, y' understand, but there is channels for the disposal of—uh—found credit cards."

"Tell us about them."

Alison was fumbling in her purse again.

"There's no need for that," he murmured. "Between friends. Besides, it's no secret. There's a place over in New Jersey. Don't ask me where exactly, because I don't know. Some bar or other, probably. But there *is* a place. And they give you fifty bucks for every hot card and no questions asked. Then they kind of process them. You know. Move them into other areas. I don't know . . ."

All at once he was blinking vaguely, as if he felt he'd said too much.

The girls looked at one another. Emmeline was near to tears again. It looked like being an impossible task they were faced with if her father's card had met *that* fate.

But Alison was not so depressed.

"Excuse us a minute, Kevin," she said.

She drew the others to one side.

"Listen, Em," she said. "This might be the best lead yet."

"Oh?"

"Yes. Every good detective has his snitch."

"His *what?*"

"Keep your voice down, Jeannie . . . His informant. Someone in the underworld who tips him off. Or someone on the streets who knows what goes on. The detective has to pay him a little for the information he gets, of course. That's only fair. Well, listen. *I think we should make Mr. O'Connor our snitch.*"

"Seems like you've done that already," said Emmeline.

"Yes, well. What I want to know is will your father reward him properly if he comes up with something leading to the recovery of the card?"

Emmeline's eyes shone.

"Sure thing! Hey, do you think—?"

"Good! Great! That's all I needed to know. Now leave it to me."

Alison went back to the man.

"Mr. O'Connor—sir—Kevin—we're going to level with you."

"Yeah?"

He looked startled, but interested.

"Yes. There could be money in this for you. Real folding money. If you can help us."

"Kathleen, my queen, just tell yer old friend what it is you want him to do!"

"Keep your eyes and ears open. Let us know if

69

you hear of anyone picking up a card belonging to Mr. Grant—"

"*Dale G. Grant* it says on it," Emmeline added eagerly.

"It was dropped somewhere between the florist's at the corner of Madison there and the apartment building over there, corner of Park, between five and five-thirty on Monday afternoon. Have you got that?"

"I have, me darling!"

Mr. O'Connor carefully repeated the facts.

"Fine!" said Alison, who'd been scribbling on a spare leaf of her notebook. "Well, here's the number to call," she said, tearing it off. "Oh, and here—" she said, handing over another quarter. "Just a little something to show good faith."

This time Mr. O'Connor didn't demur. He kissed both the scrap of paper and the coin and dropped them into the fathomless depths of his pocket.

"Deal!" he said. Then, giving a short shuffling little dance and a twirl of the stick, he said: "Things is picking up around these parts, darn me if they ain't!"

There was a gleam in Alison's eyes as she made out yet another note, shortly afterward, on the way home for lunch.

Expenses

—it was headed.

And, underneath:

50¢ paid in cash
to informant.

"I'll expect your father to pay us back when we've cracked the case," she said to Emmeline.

"No problem!" said her friend.

Emmeline looked brighter than she'd done in the whole of the past twenty-four hours. It was understandable. There was a momentum about Alison's activities at times like these—a momentum that carried you along, buoyed you along, no matter how worried you were.

And the Top-flight Fully-automated Junior High School Girl Detective had certainly lost no time establishing her street connections.

9

Miss Haverstashe

Bert, the doorman at the Grants' building, who'd been on duty on Monday afternoon, was as fat as Frank at Aunt Beth's but much more cheerful with it. In fact, when they interviewed him after lunch that Friday, Alison mentally rated him as being about halfway between Miguel and Chuck on the Doormen's Scale. As she said to the other two girls afterward:

"If you had closed-circuit television in your lobby, Emmeline, I bet Bert would let us do our elevator performances nearly every time we asked. So long as it wasn't more than once a day. And he'd cleared it with your father first."

But, alas, for all his sympathy and goodwill, Bert wasn't able to help them much.

Sure, he'd been on duty at the time. And sure, he remembered Mr. Grant entering the building that afternoon.

"I mean who wouldn't? Your father's kind of on the small side and that was one big bunch of carnations he'd got there. I mean I had to look very close to make sure who was behind it. I mean you never know. Sneak thieves'll try all sorts of dodges and disguises to get inside an apartment building."

But no. He hadn't seen Mr. Grant drop anything on his way through the lobby, or anybody pick anything up.

"Your father did inquire Monday evening, you know, and we went through all this then. *And* the day after. We all searched every possible place, and not just me. The janitor, the cleaners, everybody. If he'd dropped it here we'd have found it, don't worry."

This was Bert's polite way of saying they were wasting their time and his, and they were just thanking him with equal politeness when Emmeline nudged Alison and said in an anxious whisper:

"Oh-oh! Don't mention anything about the card to *her,* for heaven's sakes!"

"Who?" Alison asked, looking around.

The lobby seemed deserted.

But it was Bert who answered the question, without realizing it.

He had stepped smartly to the door and was opening it for a tall, ungainly elderly woman.

"Afternoon, Miss Haverstashe! Had a nice lunch?"

"I never eat in the middle of the day, Bert, you know that!" the woman replied, in a high wobbly chuckling voice, like a turkey's. "And if I may say so, it wouldn't do you any harm to miss lunch a few times."

She prodded at Bert's belt with a long finger that

looked all the longer for being enclosed in a bright yellow woolen glove.

"Come on, quick!" whispered Emmeline. "Before she sees me."

She drew Alison and Jeannie toward the elevator and stabbed the UP button.

"Oh, come on! come on!" she muttered at the closed doors.

"Is that the *same* Haverstashe?" Alison asked, turning to look curiously at the tall figure that still bent over Bert.

The woman looked very dowdy to be a relative of the great J. Hickory Haverstashe. Her long, old-fashioned, blue gabardine raincoat was almost as shapeless as Kevin O'Connor's pants, though a lot cleaner. Her thin ankles were covered with brown lisle stockings that sagged and concertinaed slightly. And she had huge feet inside what appeared to be a pair of men's heavy-duty tan brogues.

"It's his sister," Emmeline murmured. "She lives here. In fact we got to know of the apartment through her, when we first came to live in New York."

"She sounds kind of—well—jolly?" said Jeannie.
"Yeah. Jolly."

She was right. "Jolly" was the only word for that high, bubbling, chuckling laugh that arose from the doorway.

"Oh, she's all right," said Emmeline. "But she's such a blabbermouth. She'd be sure to tell her brother if he should call. And then Daddy *would* be in trouble . . . Oh, come on, come on! What's *wrong* with this elevator?"

"Might Bert mention it?" Alison asked, glancing again toward the pair in the doorway.

"No," said Emmeline. "He's been warned not to breathe a word of it to Miss Haverstashe. They *all* have . . . uh-uh! Here she comes. Look—let's pretend we're going out, after all. Make like we're in a hurry."

But they were too late to get into their stride.

"Emmeline!" cried Miss Haverstashe, her light-gray eyes bulging behind the plain gold-rimmed glasses. "And your *friends!*" Her long, scraggy neck was like a turkey's, too, the flesh wrinkled and purple-tinged. And she had two huge, jutting, yellow teeth that could easily have been mistaken for a beak, in a dim light. "I was *hoping* I'd see you today."

"Well we *are* rather in a hurry, Miss Haverstashe," mumbled Emmeline.

"I'm sure you are, my dear! Off to meet your agent, I suppose?"

That pulled Emmeline up.

"Agent? Well, no . . . *Agent,* Miss Haverstashe?"

"Good. I shouldn't like to hold up a business appointment. So sit down a minute, my dears." She patted the bench in front of the elevator bank. "Surely you can spare your keenest fan that much time?"

"Fan, Miss Haverstashe?"

Emmeline looked absolutely bewildered. Jeannie had already taken a seat, staring fascinated at the wrinkled, bobbing throat that reared from the raincoat collar. And Alison was curious also. If J. Hick-

76

ory Haverstashe was likely to cause big trouble if their investigations weren't completed in time, it would be as well to get acquainted with his sister. She seemed a very friendly old girl, if a little crazy.

"Yes! Fan!" Miss Haverstashe playfully flipped Emmeline's shoulder with a long, limp, yellow-clad hand. "Stop acting modest! I hear you're a television star now. You and—" The eyes bulged again, as she peered at Jeannie and Alison. "Why!" she crowed. "I do believe these are your co-stars! Are they?"

Alison stared hard at her. But the woman wasn't kidding. Nothing but a girlish—an *old-fashioned* girlish—innocent goodwill shone from those eyes.

"Well, yes," murmured Emmeline. "But—"

"Your father was telling me about it the other day. Isn't it *wonderful?* I nearly *cried* with joy for you, my dear!"

Alison could believe that, too. Two large tears were already beginning to slide under the gold frames and down the long purplish cracks at the side of the mouth.

"Well—" Emmeline began again, blushing slightly and giving her companions an uneasy glance.

"Nothing delights me more, I can tell you, than to hear of a young gal making her way in the world. Correction!" Miss Haverstashe flipped the tears away with a twitch of the yellow fingertips. "Something does delight me more. To hear of *three* young gals making their way in the world." She bent forward. "Congratulations, my dears! What pretty hair! You're sisters, aren't you?"

While Alison and Jeannie nodded (and even the older girl was feeling dazed by this gush of praise and good wishes) Emmeline tried to explain.

"Miss Haverstashe, did you *see* the program last night?"

At once, the light went from the woman's eyes. She dipped her head and shuffled her feet and sighed.

"No. I'm sorry. My brother refuses to—I—I don't have a television. My eyesight, you know. And I'm afraid I go to bed very early on account of my blood pressure." Then she lifted her head and the teeth broke out in another wide smile. "But I'm so thrilled by your success. I'm sure it must have been a splendid performance."

"Well—"

This time it was Alison who tried to break the news. But the woman was gushing on, and now she had a more earnest look on her face.

"But take a tip from me, girls: be careful! Don't let anyone try to take over *all* your business control, especially when you get to Hollywood. I know you're minors, and I know your father will do his best to handle all business matters on your behalf, Emmeline. But always reserve final control. In fact if you haven't done so already, make sure you get a good agent—a *woman* agent. Promise?"

"Well—" Emmeline began yet again.

"Promise!" said Alison, giving her a nudge and standing up. After all, this could go on all afternoon and they had work to do. "It's been nice talking to you, Miss Haverstashe."

"Oh—do you really have to go now? I thought

you might like to come up to my apartment and have tea and tell me about the program."

"No—we have to be getting along," said Emmeline.

"Well, do feel free to stop by, won't you? Any time, any day, before seven-thirty. If I'm in, of course." She giggled. "And I'll give you a preview of *my* performance."

"Yours, Miss Haverstashe?"

"Well, nothing so glamorous as yours, of course. It's just a hat I'm making. For the Easter Parade next weekend. My brother has promised to be back in time to escort me there."

The mention, even indirectly, of J. Hickory Haverstashe cast a shadow over the scene, like a gallows tree. Alison remembered suddenly that they really did have work to do, and not *too* much time to do it in.

"Some other time, Miss Haverstashe. We'd love to," she said.

"What pretty hair!" Miss Haverstashe called after them. "All three of you!" Then she sighed, sadly, harshly, and said in a lower voice, but one that still carried as far as the door: "And how lucky they are!"

10
Rollo and the Dogs

Miss Haverstashe wouldn't have thought they were all that lucky if she'd followed them around.

For now, as the afternoon approached zero hour, the rush hour, the time when the card had been lost, the girls concentrated on passers-by. And the closer it got to that hour the faster the passers tended to go by. In fact, *passers*-by became quite the wrong word for them. *Hurriers*-by would have been more appropriate. Or *bustlers*-by. Or *tramplers*-by. Or *hurtlers*-by. Or—sad to report—*cussers*-by.

"I think New Yorkers *really are* the rudest people on earth!" Emmeline kept quavering, with a look in her eyes that was beginning to suggest she wouldn't find Cleveland such a bad move, after all.

"I know what you mean!" Alison replied, one time, after nearly being stiff-armed off the sidewalk by a little old lady not much bigger than Jeannie.

"It's not that we don't ask *politely!*" complained Jeannie, who was beginning to look five years older and harder already.

But it seemed that no matter how they made their approach, the result was always the same: the brush-off.

Alison soon realized that it wasn't worth making notes of their questions and answers this time. If she *had* taken the trouble, those short exchanges would only have looked like this:

"Excuse me—"

"Nuh-huh!"

Or:

"I'm sorry to—"

"Outadaway!"

Or:

"We're hoping you'll be able to—"

"I already gave!"

Or:

"Sir, do you usually come this way at around this—"

"I don't know what your racket is, kid, but if you don't get lost I'll call a cop!"

Or:

"Look, this won't take a minute, but—"

"Too long! So long!"

Or:

"Please will you help us? We—"

"Giddoutahere!"

And those were only a few of the least rude responses. Nobody stopped to listen properly. Only about half even slackened their pace. And very few indeed so much as looked at them.

"It isn't as if it was raining!" moaned Emmeline, around five-fifteen.

"It doesn't even look like rain!" said Jeannie, staggering a little as she rubbed the tip of one shoe against the calf of her other leg, after someone had stepped on her toes *as well as* cussing her. "I hope it does though. I hope it pours, before they get home, and they've forgotten their keys and can't get in, and—"

"Now *here's* somebody who might be able to help!" said Alison, brightening. "Why didn't we think of him before?"

She was nodding toward the Park Avenue end of the street, where what seemed at first to be a miniature cattle stampede was in progress. Instead of a herd of cows, however, it was a pack of dogs—all yapping and prancing delightedly around the heels of a tall, broad-shouldered young man with black hair and long black mustaches.

He was walking at a slow and stately pace toward the girls, a bunch of leashes in each hand. His eyes and brow and indeed the whole of his face were remarkably composed and placid, but a close observer would have marveled at the activity of his fingers as he manipulated those leashes: tightening here, slackening there, twitching, tugging, sending out silent messages to the animals at the other end.

Mr. McNair had once said:

"It's a pleasure to watch Rollo steer those dogs through the rush-hour crowd. He does it all with his fingers. All the way from Lexington to the park. Marvelous!"

"Well, of course, he *is* a musician," Mrs. McNair had replied. "Or studying to be one. Their brains are in their fingers, you know."

82

Anyway, that was Rollo—student of piano, harpsichord, and other keyboard instruments at the Juilliard, and dog-walker extraordinary in his spare time. Also something of a hero to the neighborhood kids, as well as to the dogs—and never more so to those three girls than at this particular time.

"Oh, Rollo! Hi!"

Rollo gave them a placid nod, and for a moment it looked as if he too was going to keep on walking past them. But in his case this was excusable, because, as his busy fingers indicated, he'd just got his dogs flowing smoothly in a delicate arpeggio passage that was nicely counterpointing the hurrying human feet all around them. As soon as he realized the girls were flagging him down, however, he called a halt.

"Kah!" he seemed to say, in what was nothing more than a gentle bark itself. Then his fingers went still and stiff and the dogs stopped—some sniffing, some whining impatiently, some taking advantage of the opportunity to scratch themselves.

There were, on this particular afternoon, seven of them: a chow, an Afghan hound, two poodles, a Pekingese, an Old English sheepdog, and a beagle. Only Rollo could have *walked* such an assortment, let alone brought them quietly to a standstill so swiftly.

"So," he said, after clearing his throat in an effort to get back from the language of music and dogs to the regular day-to-day human sort, "so how are things with you?"

"Awful!" said Alison.

"Simply awful!" cut in Emmeline.

"Couldn't be worser!" added Jeannie, switching from rubbing her toes to patting the sheepdog.

"But we're hoping you may be able to help, Rollo," said Alison.

Then she told him.

He listened carefully—his smooth, untroubled brow and clear, steady blue eyes bent courteously on the speaker—only interrupting to give an occasional warning woof or growl to one or other of the dogs.

"And since you come along here most every weekday at this time—"

"*Every* weekday," Rollo corrected her, in a polite manner. "Rain, shine . . . yeah . . . including Monday of course . . . hmm . . . Someone picking something up, you say? . . . Well, now . . ."

He was frowning thoughtfully.

The girls held their breath.

One of the poodles yawned.

The beagle flapped its ears impatiently.

"Well, let me tell ya," Rollo murmured. "I remember that afternoon specially—"

"Good! Great!" said Alison.

"No. Not so good. Not so great. Like I remember it specially because Humphrey here"—he nodded at the Old English sheepdog—"was playing at trying to trip up the passers-by—"

"Good for you, Humphrey!" said Jeannie, giving the dog a pat. "Attaboy!"

"And I was so busy watching him," Rollo continued, "that I just didn't see much of what was going on around us. *But,*" he said, causing the girls' drooping spirits to rise, "I must have been here right at the time you mention, because one of the passers-by Humphrey nearly tripped was your old—your father, Emmeline. Carrying flowers, right?"

"Oh yes! Right!"

"Right. Because what made Humphrey nearly trip *him* was I think the dog kinda liked the smell of those chrysanthemums—"

"Carnations."

"Whatever. And wanted to get closer." Rollo nodded. "Maybe that's when your father dropped the card. Shying away from Humphrey. That what you getting at?"

"Well—"

"But somebody *bending down?* Yeah. Just a bit farther along. Now you mention it I do have a shadowy kind of recollection."

"Oh, Rollo, *think,* please! Who? *Think!"*

"I'm trying. But like all I have in my mind is this stooping figure, with people having to step around it, just across by the corner there, and me thinking I'll keep the dogs over here, one obstruction is enough." He looked around at them. "I usually cross at that point, you see."

Alison felt her heart throbbing.

This was because "that point"—and the "corner there"—was where Mr. Grant must have walked, right after leaving the florist's.

But Rollo was shaking his head.

"Sorry!" he said. "It just won't come. Maybe the details didn't even register. But if I do happen to remember something—"

Which is when the alarm went off.

Humphrey seemed to have been enjoying Jeannie's attentions, because when she was through patting him and on the point of transferring her interest to the Afghan, he turned his great, shaggy, noble head abruptly. Jeannie, mistaking this for a snap, swung her hand back out of reach with equal abruptness. This caused the shoulder-strap to jerk and the purse to clump against Emmeline's legs—and that set off the alarm.

But the chain reaction didn't end there, by any means. The alarm startled the dogs and particularly the beagle. Whether the beagle was really as startled as he made out—enough to raise a high squeal and nip the chow's tail—is another matter. Maybe he was just bored and, like all bored beagles, quick to seize an excuse for a bit of hectic sport.

Anyway, from then on the situation was explosive. The dogs barked, yelped, leaped, spun. Rollo was suddenly transformed into the Maypole of a mad dance. The sidewalk cleared as if by magic, all around him and his dogs, and hurriers-by suddenly became stoppers-by—fascinated by the spectacle.

Rollo rose to the occasion, after the first shock. He rattled off a series of quick authoritative barks that sounded like machine-gun fire. He twitched and tugged those leashes with all the skill and urgency of a marionette master who suddenly finds his puppets running out of control. It became one of the great solo performances of all time, in that greatest theater of all time—The Streets of New York.

Then Alison saw her chance.

She realized that there could now be no hope of

getting Rollo to remember anything useful *that* afternoon. So she did the next best thing. She looked around and saw that for the moment anyway those rush-hour people were no longer in a hurry. For a brief spell they had paused, had opened their eyes and maybe their hearts. They were a happy contented captive audience.

"Come on, girls!" she said. "Let's ask around *now!*"

And they did. Instead of taking the *hat* around for contributions (which is what some of those hard-nosed people suspected, judging from their looks when the girls tapped their arms) they took the *notebook* around for possible witnesses.

Well, this time the responses were a lot less rude. People were rather puzzled perhaps, by the nature of the question. Some were even a little miffed to have their attention distracted from Rollo's magnificent efforts to quell the canine whirlwind. But at least they tried to give some sort of answer.

Yet still it was no good.

Nobody remembered having seen anybody pick up anything from that sidewalk Monday afternoon. Out of all the people present, only one person had come near to that and, judging from the sweat on his broad smooth brow, he'd be in no mood even to attempt to answer their question for days.

"Come on," said Alison finally, as Rollo regained full control and the crowd began to break up into its flying particles once more. "Let's see if there's been a call from our snitch."

But when they got to the McNair apartment they

found there had been no call for Alison at all that afternoon, and that seemed to be that. The girls split
up to get ready for their evening meals. Nevertheless,
as Alison said:

"We may not have gotten any positive results, but
we've sure covered a lot of ground."

Even Emmeline had to agree that, for the first
day, they hadn't done so badly in their investigations.
She went away looking reasonably confident.

That was *before* supper, of course.

After supper, Emmeline was back at the McNairs'
apartment with tears in her eyes and her hair all
disheveled.

"What's wrong *now,* Em?" Alison asked, feeling
quite alarmed at the look on her friend's face.

"Oh, Ally!" cried Emmeline. "It's getting worse!
Daddy came home from work looking *haggard!* . . .
You see, the latest list has come in, and—and there
are twelve more items on it. The thief has bought at
least twelve more things with Daddy's card, just in
one day, yesterday."

"But—"

"Nothing over one hundred dollars again. But it
adds up to hundreds. To seven hundred and ninety-
six dollars, to be exact!"

At the mention of such a sum, Alison stopped trying to look cool. Her face must have registered
nearly as much horror as Emmeline's, because that
girl went on:

"Yes! I know! Daddy says that if J. Hickory Haverstashe was dead and not just in San Francisco
he'd be turning in his grave!"

11
The Squad Room

Jeannie's angry wish for rain was answered generously—so generously that she began to boast about it, saying, "I still must have a lot of my witchcraft powers left." Rather spoiling that boast, however, was the fact that the wish needed seventeen or eighteen hours to take effect. It wasn't until around ten o'clock on Saturday morning that the rain came down.

When it did, though, it came down in style: torrential at first, with thunder and lightning, easing off only into a steady downpour that lasted all day and into the evening. There could have been no legwork most of Saturday, unless those legs had had webbed feet at the end of them.

Fortunately, the girls had managed to tie up a few loose ends in the first dull and threatening but dry hour of the day. They had at last got to interview the doormen they had missed the day before. The results were only too predictable. Three fierce *zilches* went down in Alison's notebook. But, as she said when the rain started:

"At least we're up to date with the legwork for the

time being. Now we can stay indoors and concentrate on the background to the case."

Her idea of background work was turning her bedroom into a kind of police department squad room and examining the crime in all its details. For this, she would dearly have liked all the technological equipment she'd seen in various television dramas. Projector units, to throw onto a screen blown-up images of clues and suspects. Large ceiling-to-floor glass panels with street plans painted on them and a grease pencil for her to sketch out new moves. A telephone with a box attachment and a switch that could activate a loudspeaker, so that everyone in the room could hear what was being said at the other end. Things like that: toys that the Great Detective and all his TV rivals, from McGarrett of "Hawaii Five-O" to Barnaby Jones played with on the family screens, week in, week out.

What Alison actually had to make do with were: a battered blackboard and easel from Jeannie's room, with a set of broken chalks; a tattered street-map of New York, borrowed from Mr. McNair's den and pinned to the wall in the space vacated by Thursday's torn-down poster; and a box of pins with colored glass heads.

"O.K.," she said, when everything was in place, with Emmeline, Jeannie, and Norton sitting on the bed facing her, while she stood by the blackboard. "First—the card itself. Describe it."

"Well—er—well, it's just a credit card really. You know."

"No, I don't know. What does it have on it?"

"Well—er—it says Newcharge, of course. And it has Daddy's name on it, printed, and—"

"Yeah. That. What does it say? 'Mr. Grant'? His initials? His full names? What?"

"No. Just 'Dale G. Grant.' No *Mr.* or *Ms.* or anything on Newcharge cards. I know that because there was a big row when the cards were first designed. Somebody said they couldn't put *Miss* or *Mrs.* these days, it had to be *Ms.*, and J. Hickory Haverstashe fired him because he *hates* Women's Lib things. And—"

"Creep!"

"Be quiet, Jeannie. Go on, Emmeline. So what happened then?"

"Well for once Daddy really pleased J. Hickory Haverstashe. He said why not drop all the titles? Don't have *Mr., Mrs., Miss,* or *Ms.*—just the name. And so they did. I think it saved a bit on printing costs too, or something, and—"

"Never mind that."

Alison was busy chalking up a picture of the card: the usual oblong shape with rounded corners, with the word NEWCHARGE across the top, and the name DALE G. GRANT in the bottom left corner.

"Number?"

"Well, there is one, of course. And I know it begins one-zero-zero. But I couldn't say exactly what it is right now."

"No matter."

Alison made a rough hieroglyphic squiggle where she thought the number would be.

"Much more important, this next question. So

think. Is there your father's signature on the card?"

"Oh sure! I don't have to think. I know. Daddy said whoever's got the card is also guilty of forgery, because he's been copying the signature to put on the sales slips."

"Forgery too, huh?" murmured Alison, a gleam in her eyes.

"He isn't a very good forger," said Emmeline. "But he doesn't have to be. Nobody bothers to check the signature very closely in the stores, especially for items under one hundred dollars."

"Right," said Alison. "And that brings me to the procedure. Let's take what happens in the stores first. O.K.? Imagine I'm the perpetrator and I have your father's card and I'm in a store and I'm buying something."

So saying, she hunched her shoulders, and screwed up her mouth, and darted her eyes from side to side, and shuffled to the dressing table in so sinister a fashion that Jeannie gave a little squeal of delighted fright. Norton, made of tougher material, narrowed his eyes and thrust forward his head—probably thinking that Alison might be about to embark on his favorite pouncing game.

"Oh, Alison!" said Emmeline, smiling in spite of her troubles. "I'm sure the thief knows better than to draw attention to himself like that."

"Well, whatever. What happens now?"

"Well, he hands the card to the clerk, instead of money, and the clerk registers the name and number and gets the customer to sign a sales slip."

"Tell us about the sales slip."

"Well . . . like it's a sales slip . . . I mean it says what the article is and the price and the tax. And it has the name and address of the store on it. And—well—a sales slip."

"But the customer signs it—right? In this case 'Dale G. Grant'—right?"

"Right. And there are three copies. At least three. A top and carbons. And the customer gets one copy for his receipt, and the store keeps one—at least one—and the third is sent to Newcharge."

"I'd like one of those cards," said Jeannie. "I'd buy all sorts of things and—"

"Don't be childish!" snapped Alison. "The customer has to pay real money in the end. Right, Emmeline?"

"Right. Every month, the people at Newcharge add up how much the customer owes and send him a bill."

"I'd still like one of those cards," said Jeannie stubbornly. "Daddy would pay the account."

"That's exactly why minors aren't allowed to have credit cards, honey," said Emmeline, in her gentle, patient voice.

"Ha!"

Alison gave such a loud cry that it cut through the drumming of the rain on the windows and closely competed with a clap of thunder outside. Norton went under the bed.

"What—what is it, Ally?"

"That's just narrowed down our search," she said. "At least we know that whoever's using that card so freely, and getting away with it, isn't a kid."

Emmeline sighed.

94

"Fine!" she said. "That narrows it down from nine million suspects to about six or seven million."

"Well, it's something," growled Alison.

Then she crisped up again.

"So. We know what happens at the store end of the operation. What happens at the Newcharge offices? They get the sales slips. Then what? Apart from billing the customer every month."

"Well, they pay the stores however much the purchases cost," said Emmeline. "And what's more, they pay them right away. As soon as they get the slip with the customer's signature. That's what's different about Newcharge. Quick service. It's a new company and it's what makes stores like to do business with them. Especially small stores. They don't have to wait so long for their money."

"I see," said Alison. "That's why we're getting such fast information about what the thief is buying."

Emmeline sighed again.

"Right," she said. "But of course some of the bigger stores aren't in such a hurry. They don't bother to send in the slips for a week or so sometimes."

Alison nodded.

"So the damage could be worse. The thief could have bought more than we know about yet."

"Much more," said Emmeline gloomily.

"Gosh!" said Jeannie—to whom last night's mention of seven hundred and ninety-six dollars had conjured up visions of all the money in the Bank of America.

But Alison was looking pleased.

"Good!" she said. "Great!"

"What?" yelped Emmeline.

Alison blinked.

"Sorry. I didn't mean about more purchases than we know of. I was thinking back. Listen, Em. Does your father have details of all the purchases *so far?* Names and addresses of stores. At home, I mean?"

Emmeline nodded.

"Yes," she said, very definitely. "In fact he daren't keep the list anyplace else *but* home. He's still hoping the thief will be caught before J. Hickory Haverstashe gets back. Meanwhile, the fewer people at work who know about it, the better. He says it's worse than school for tattletales."

"Good!" said Alison again. "So do you think you could get a copy?"

"Of the *list?*"

"Yes. And soon. Right now."

"Well—sure. I don't see why not. As soon as the rain slackens off—"

"Never mind the rain! This is urgent. You want us to track down the card and the perpetrator, don't you?"

"Sure, but I don't see what—"

"The list, dummy, will give us the addresses of the stores he's already hit with the stolen card. Right? So if we stick one of these red pins into every one of those places—on the map here"—Alison crossed to the wall and thumped the street plan—"why, then we'll be able to see just where he's been operating, and if there's a pattern."

Emmeline was already on her way. Her face was glowing with revived hope.

96

12
The Colored Flies

"There *is* a pattern! See?"

Alison's expression was a mixture of pleasure and pride as she waved the list at the street map, late Saturday afternoon.

She had just stuck the last red pin in place, and there they now were—all sixteen of them—in a glittering cluster of sparks.

"Like a bombshell!" murmured Emmeline, with deep feeling, no doubt thinking of the damage to family security they represented.

"Most of them within ten blocks of this room," said Alison, her own mind running on more practical lines.

This seemed to bring Emmeline back to the immediate realities of their task.

"With just a few of them scattered downtown and farther·up on the East Side," she observed.

"To me," said Jeannie, "it looks like a splash of blood with little drops all around it. You know?"

"Yik!" went Emmeline.

"You *would* think of something like that!" Alison told her sister. Then she turned to Emmeline. "But anyway, there it is." She was looking pleased again. "And already it's beginning to tell us something about the perpetrator."

Emmeline was fingering the damp wisps at the ends of her hair. The rain still drummed against the windows. She was frowning.

"Oh?" she asked hesitantly.

"Sure!" said Alison. "It tells us he probably lives around here. Right?"

Emmeline slowly nodded. But she continued to frown.

"I guess so—only . . ."

She stepped closer to the map and peered at the location of a solitary pin, down toward the bottom left of the sheet. Then she gave a little start as she read the words under the pin.

"Gosh! Oh *no!*"

"What?"

"This one. See where it is? I've just realized."

"What? Penn Station? So what?" Alison glanced at the list. "It's where he bought a real leather wallet, twenty-seven dollars plus tax, in one of the stores they have inside the station. They'll probably never remember him in a busy place like that. But that's no reason for looking so worried, Em." She gave the main cluster of pins a light flick with her fingernails, producing a faint tinny snickering sound. "Plenty more places for us to inquire at. Places where they might easily recall him stopping by to use the card."

Emmeline was shaking her head.

"No. No. It wasn't that." She sighed. "Ally—don't

you know where the trains *go* to from Penn Station?"

"Sure. Long Island. Our Uncle Brad lives at—"

"No. Not just Long Island. Where do they *also* go to . . . ?"

"Well, Washington, I guess. And Philadelphia. And—oh!"

Alison broke off, suddenly looking as worried as her friend.

"Yes!" said Emmeline. " 'Oh' is the word!"

"What are you two talking about?" said Jeannie, beginning to sound annoyed.

"It's the station for trains to New Jersey, Jeannie," Emmeline explained. "And—well—don't you see? It could have been his last stop, after buying all the other stuff, on his way to sell the card to that organization. The one that Mr. O'Connor was telling us—"

"Hold it! Hold it!" Alison was looking at the list. When she raised her head it was with a big smile. "Emmeline, it's O.K. Really. Forget it. That wallet was bought on Wednesday. *Before* most of these other items."

Emmeline took a deep breath. Her face cleared a little. Then the frown came back as she stared at the lone pin.

"I wonder why he did go all the way down there, though? There are plenty of leather-goods stores around here."

"I know!" said Jeannie. "Maybe he was going to visit his uncle in New Jersey. Maybe the wallet was a gift for his uncle. He must be a sort of *kind* man, mustn't he? To think of taking an expensive gift like that to his poor old—"

"Jeannie!" Alison's voice had a stern ring. "Don't

get carried away, kid. Don't get soft on this creep.
He's a thief, remember. A forger. A—a *perpetrator!*"

"Yeah," said Jeannie, rather awed. "Sorry, Ally."
Then her eyes widened. "Penn Station? Maybe he
went to the circus. Isn't that there? Right over the
station, in Madison Square Garden? Maybe—"

"So now he's an animal lover!" snapped Alison.
"Or a clown! Or—oh, what does it matter, all this
Penn Station, Penn Station? The main thing is—"

"Oh-oh!" Emmeline snapped her fingers. "I just
thought of something."

Now she was looking almost as distressed as she
had at the idea of New Jersey.

"What?"

"Macy's."

"Huh?"

"Macy's is there," said Emmeline, stabbing a finger
at a spot just to the right of the pin. "Just around
the corner from the station. I've been there often."

"So?"

"So I bet he went on a shopping spree there. Oh
gosh, of course he would! And I bet he bought *thousands* of things, in all the different departments. It—
it's the biggest store in the *world*. And—and of
course they're not in such a big hurry as some of the
small places. They won't have sent in the Newcharge
slips yet. There's probably"—she swallowed, as her
voice began to falter—"there's probably a whole
stack of items to add to the list. Already. From that
one store alone!"

Alison shrugged. She looked worried, but not
downcast.

"Well, no sweat, Em. Look. As soon as these places are open again, Monday morning, we'll start checking around. We'll go to every single store on the list—at least all those in this area—and we'll ask around. *Someone* should remember him."

But Alison was wrong that time. The perpetrator was a very cunning operator, whoever he was. He had taken care to make his illegal purchases either in large stores which were busy all the time, or in small stores only when they *were* busy.

The result was that Monday's investigations drew blank after blank. Sure, they got lectures on just how many kinds of credit cards there were, even before you got around to talking about individual holders' names. They were also given statistics—like "how many people step up to this counter, *per hour,* every day of the week." And in store after store the clerks, instead of answering their questions, fired questions back at them. Like:

"What kind of a joke *is* this?"

Or:

"Is this some kinda crazy school assignment?"

Or:

"If this is on the level, it's a job for the police, not kids like you, right? I mean just what would you do if I *could* remember the looks of the guy who purchased the watch, which I can't, we sell dozens like it every day, huh? What would your next step *be?*"

Finally, at the fourteenth store, late that afternoon, they were ready to call it a day, a *lousy* day. It was a sporting-goods store on Lexington, and as they entered it, Alison's wilting hopes revived a little. It was a big place, true, with a dozen or so clerks, but, as Alison said, after glancing again at the list:

"Surely someone doesn't come in to buy flies *every* day."

Jeannie's drawn face broke into a grin then, despite her tiredness.

"You're kidding, Ally. *Flies?*"

"It says it here and—sure! Look! Staring at you!"

She pointed to a display case in front of a counter, gleaming and glowing with rows and rows of small colored winged insects.

"*Artificial* flies!" said Emmeline. She looked around, noticing nets, rods, reels. "For fishing with. Of course!"

"They're lovely!" said Jeannie, crouching forward until her nose was pressed against the glass.

"Do you want to buy some or not?" asked a tall thin man behind the counter.

He had a face a bit like a trout's himself.

"Well, not exactly, sir," said Alison, casting up at him a smile as radiant and beautiful as the very best of those flies. "We're wondering if you could tell us if you remember who bought"—she glanced at the list—"a set of fifteen of these, last Thursday."

She smiled again.

The fish man was not tempted. He bit, all right, but it was more of a snapping at thin air.

"Miss!" His eyes bulged. "I don't know what your game is, but this"—he tapped the case—"is one of our best-selling lines. Every day we do about five hundred dollars' worth of business in flies in the mail-order department alone! And almost as much as

102

that over the counter here toward weekends. Now if you don't wish to buy, please stand aside. As you see, there are already three *serious* customers waiting behind you, and it's only Monday!"

Feeling crushed and sore, Alison retreated. Her cheeks were hot and her eyes were angry.

"Oh, let's go home!" said Jeannie. "I want to eat!"

"Well, we *tried,* Ally," murmured Emmeline.

"I wouldn't mind," growled Alison, "but they've got to *lecture* you all the time, some people!"

"I know. But it is unusual, I suppose—our request. Maybe when he's through serving those three—"

"Nargh!" Alison had started to head for the door, past another long counter in the fishing section. "He'd only start over again. Sneering and—and—*lecturing.* Store clerks are just a bunch of frustrated teachers, if you ask me. They—"

Then she stopped, unable to believe her ears.

Not more than three or four yards away, another clerk was handing back a credit card to a customer and saying:

"Have a nice day, Mr. Grant. And good fishing!"

13
The Suspect

"Did you hear what I heard?" asked Emmeline, in a shocked whisper.

"What's wrong?" said Jeannie, looking up at the other two.

"First the flies," murmured Alison, staring at the man who was walking very slowly to the door. He was carrying a long, thin wrapped package upright against his chest, while he replaced the credit card in his wallet. "Then he couldn't resist buying a new fishing rod. . . . Oh, but he's cool!"

The man had paused near the door. He had finally stowed away his wallet (*"The* wallet," Alison told herself. "The one he bought at Penn Station!") with the card ("Emmeline's *father's* card!") now safe in his breast pocket. ("Trust a thief to make sure *he* doesn't get ripped off!")

He was tall and quite well dressed ("They usually are, the clever ones!") in a tan raincoat and neatly pressed gray pants with fashionably flared bottoms. His shoes were of the expensive kind, too, made of glossy chestnut-colored patent leather, with gold buckles.

"What are you staring at that man for?"

"Sh!" both older girls hissed at Jeannie.

The man didn't seem to have heard. His fresh-complexioned face continued to wear the blank, contented, completely tranquil expression it had worn all along, as he gave his collar a tug and stepped through the doorway.

"He doesn't *look* like a thief," said Emmeline.

"They never do, the really cool ones," said Alison. "Come on."

"But what shall we *do*, Ally?" asked Emmeline, as they hurried out, with the still bewildered Jeannie following them.

All at once, the words of the man in the watch store had taken on a new importance.

What indeed would their next step be?

"I'm not sure," said Alison grimly, moving along the crowded sidewalk as quickly and unobtrusively as possible. "But I do know what we must *not* do."

"What's that?"

"Lose sight of him. If he slows, we slow. If he runs, we run. If he goes in a store, we wait. If he catches a cab—hey! How much money do you have in your purse, Emmeline?"

"Oh, about three dollars. But—"

"That should do it. If he catches a cab, we do too. I always wanted to get in one and tell the driver, 'Follow that cab!'"

"Would someone mind telling *me*—"

"He's the one, Jeannie!" said Emmeline. "He's the

—the perpetrator. Didn't you hear what the clerk said when he handed him his card back?"

"Shouldn't we call a cop then?"

"No time," said Alison. "He could lose himself in this crowd by the time we explained. No. We've got to follow and hope he leads us to where he lives."

"Which looks like someplace due east," said Emmeline.

She was judging this from the way the man was walking (fast, but without panic, as if eager to get home and unwrap his latest trophy), straight across the avenues, keeping to the same side of the same street all the time.

"Wow!" gasped Jeannie. "It's making me—run out of—breath!"

"Just keep up, that's all," said Alison. "Or drop out and make your own way home. We can't afford to lose him now."

"He—he's got to stop soon," said Emmeline. "Or he'll end up in the East River."

Already they had crossed over Second Avenue.

"Maybe that's where he's going fishing," said Jeannie.

"Cut the fooling," said Alison. "This is no time for jokes. Concentrate. And—and hurry up. He's crossing to the other side of the street, see. He may be—yes!"

Suddenly she stopped.

The man had stepped around the back of a parked truck, but he didn't emerge on the sidewalk in front of it, farther along.

"He's gone in there!"

She pointed to a tall, narrow apartment building, outside of which the truck was parked.

"What now, Ally?"

"We've got to see *exactly* where he lives," said Alison, giving a little stamp of impatience. "It looks like a big building, probably hundreds of rooms in back there. Let's go."

"You mean follow him *inside?*" asked Emmeline, as they waited for a car to pass.

"Why not?"

Alison was moving forward already.

"But the doorman will stop us!"

Alison paused behind the truck and wheeled on her companions.

"Not if we act confident and just go straight in as if our aunt lived there," she said. "It's not as if we were—well—boys. And—well—our clothes—we *look* like we might have relatives in there. Now come *on,* or it'll be too late anyway."

What she meant, but hated to admit, was that they were three young schoolgirls with decent clothes, clean faces, and respectable middle-class looks. But luckily she didn't have to put this theory to the test. The doorman was too busy right then to notice them. He was a big, red-haired man, and he was stabbing an angry finger at the chest of an equally big man who was standing by the open door of the truck's cab.

"And I'm telling *you,* feller," the driver was saying, "that I don't leave this spot till I make my delivery."

"Oh *no?*"

"Oh *no!*"

"Is *that* so?"

"That *is* so!"

The girls passed into the building unseen.

And their luck held.

Their man was still in sight, waiting near the elevator bank. His face was glowing now, partly because of the brisk walk he'd had, and probably partly with boyish anticipation as he plucked at the wrapping of his latest purchase to peek inside. At any rate, he was far too interested in the contents of the package to pay any attention to the three studiously wooden-faced girls who got into the elevator with him.

He pressed the button marked 2, and Alison

stiffened further. The ride would be shorter than she'd expected. Soon now, very soon, they would have his exact address.

"Hey!"

Someone yelled, a latecomer probably, but the doors were already closing. The man was still too preoccupied with his package to pay any attention. Jeannie, public-spirited as ever, stretched to the OPEN button, but Alison quietly slapped her sister's hand down. She frowned and shook her head. The elevator rose.

The doors opened at Floor 2 almost immediately. The man stepped out, humming under his breath. The girls followed. He walked past several doors, then stopped in front of one and took out a key.

Praying that the other two would follow her lead, Alison continued along the corridor, without faltering, as cool and casual as the man himself had been in the sporting-goods store.

She noted the number, though: 205.

When they had turned the first corner, she stopped.

The others bumped into her.

It was so quiet she could hear their quick heavy breathing. But it was the slam of the door she was waiting for, and the slide of a bolt.

These sounds came.

"Good!" she whispered. "Now we know where he hangs out. Now we can take our time deciding what to do next."

"I think we ought to call Daddy right away," said Emmeline.

"Yeah," said Jeannie. "He looked a very strong man."

"Well, maybe you're right," said Alison, reluctant to leave the final showdown to others. "But—"

"*There y'are!*"

That hoarse harsh voice wasn't what made them spin around as fast as they did. A split second before it, there had been a bursting noise, as someone pushed open the fire staircase door behind them.

It was the red-haired doorman. His face was crimson and shining with sweat.

"Didn't you hear me? What you doing here? Who are ya? Huh?"

He must have finished his fight with the truck driver just in time to see them enter the elevator. It had obviously been his yell they'd heard.

"It's—well—we—"

Alison gave Emmeline a sharp "leave-this-to-me" nudge.

"It's a criminal," she said, looking up at the man with her gravest expression. "We've followed him all the way from Lexington."

"A *what?*"

"A criminal. A perp—a man who's been passing himself off as Mr. Grant and using his credit card."

At the mention of the nature of the crime, the doorman began to look uneasy.

"You sure about this? Mr.—Mr. Grant, you say? He's been using Mr. Grant's *credit card?*"

Three earnest faces nodded up at him.

"Right!"

"Correct!"

"We *saw* him!"

The doorman frowned. His chunky features began to crumple into a look of sheer dumb perplexity. As if that truck driver hadn't been enough for one afternoon, now there was this!

That was what he seemed to be thinking.

"Well—where did he go?"

"In there. Room 205."

"You actually saw him going *in* there?"

"Right. He's in there now."

Now the doorman looked convinced.

"Gee!" he murmured.

He scratched his chin. His small eyes began to dart uneasily from side to side. He too was obviously wondering what to do next.

Alison decided to prod him along in the right direction. A note of urgency seemed to be the right thing to introduce at this point, she thought. Then she had an inspiration.

"And that package," she said, partly to Emmeline and Jeannie. "It needn't have been a fishing pole, you know. It was a sporting-goods store, remember. It could have been a shotgun, a hunting rifle."

The man gave a start.

Alison had no means of knowing all this. She was only hoping that the mention of firearms would be enough to strike that urgent note and so produce some quick action. But it so happened that the apartment building they were in was not far from the United Nations Headquarters. Important foreign diplomats were always passing along the street on their way to and from the UN building. This meant that at times of crisis there was always a danger of an assassination attempt—and then the whole area would be crawling with security agents.

Well, as far as the doorman knew, there was no international crisis at the moment. Yet there was always the risk that someone might start one by knocking off a foreign big shot during a quiet period. And if that happened—with the killer firing out of *this* building—the doorman who'd let him slip through would be looking for a new job. Or worse (he broke out in a fresh wave of sweat at the very thought)— they might suspect him of being an accomplice and let him rot in jail until he confessed.

The doorman groaned.

Why, oh why, had he deserted his post to argue with that dumb deliveryman?

Then the thought struck him that the truck driver might have been in on the plot, deliberately decoying him away from his post so that the hit man could get in unchallenged.

That clinched it.

"One of you—*you*—" he said to Emmeline, who was nearest, "go down the fire stairs to the first floor now. Get the super, Room 101, next the elevators. Tell him to call the police. Tell him it's a—a phony—"

"An imposter," suggested Alison.

"Yeah. Tell him to tell them that. Holed up in Room 205. And—wait—tell him to tell them the man's believed to be armed. Now go."

Emmeline went, two steps at a time, while the doorman grabbed hold of Alison and Jeannie and made them stand well back, behind him, while he kept watch on Room 205 from around the corner.

Alison barely had time to resent this before Emmeline reappeared.

"They're on their way!" she whispered. "Oh, Ally! This really *is* like on television! I hope he doesn't leave before they come."

"We can always trip him with our purses," said Jeannie, swinging hers in readiness so viciously that it started to tick.

"You'll keep well back, you hear?" grunted the doorman. "This is a job for cops. Not kids."

"Who tracked him down, I'd like to know!" said Alison angrily. "I mean—"

But by then the police had arrived—two patrolmen, fingering their gun butts—with a little man in glasses fussing behind them, asking them to keep the damage down.

"The super," said Emmeline.

Alison nodded.

She was more interested in the way the policemen were proceeding. To her, they seemed far too casual.

One of them tipped back his hat and rang the bell on the door of 205.

"Yes?" came the faint response.

"May we talk with you a minute?"

"Who is it?"

"Police."

There came the sound of a bolt, a chain.

Now the policemen had stiffened. They stood with their legs apart, balanced, one man on each side of the door. Their guns were being gripped now, not just fingered.

Then the door opened and the man stood there, blinking.

The doorman gasped.

The super swung around.

"I thought you said he was an imposter!"

"But he *is!*" said Emmeline.

"He's impersonating Mr. Grant," said Alison. "Search his wallet if you don't believe us, and see what it says on the credit card."

"But this *is* Mr. Grant!" howled the super. He swung back to the group in the doorway. "I'm sorry, Mr. Grant, but there's been a stupid mistake. These kids—this dummy—argh!"

Words failed the little man as he glared at the girls and the doorman, over his shoulder.

114

"Is this correct, sir?" one of the policemen was saying. "You are Mr. Grant? The tenant of this apartment?"

"Sure," said the man. "Lawrence S. Grant. Here." He pulled out his wallet. "Take a look for yourself. Credit cards, driver's license—"

"That won't be necessary, sir," said one of the cops.

"Well?" said the other, addressing the girls.

"Well," said Alison, gulping, realizing where they'd gone wrong, suddenly remembering the columns full of Grants that had confronted her whenever she'd consulted the telephone directory in the days before she'd memorized Emmeline's number. "Well first, it was all our fault, not this gentleman's . . ." She indicated the doorman, who nodded vigorously. "But you can't really blame us, because—well—you see, it's like this . . ."

Then she told them about the stolen credit card and their quest for the perpetrator.

The cops were satisfied. After peering at her closely and steadily, they seemed convinced that this was no joke—especially when Emmeline was able to produce her library card and prove that her name really was Grant.

The super was satisfied, too.

"You was only doing your job, Albert," he said, slapping the big man on the shoulder.

Only Mr. Lawrence S. Grant himself didn't look too satisfied.

"Fair enough," he said, rather grimly, nodding at each of the girls in turn. "But you could have made a few *polite* inquiries first, surely." Alison blushed, but it was Emmeline he was looking at now. "And I think your father ought to have more sense than to let three kids go around bugging people like this."

"But he doesn't know. We're—"

The man ignored her.

"I happen to know the President of Newcharge," he was saying nastily. "J. Hickory Haverstashe, right? . . . Right! And the next time I see him, I'll let him know just what I think about this!"

As the three dejected sleuths returned to the street, Jeannie put a gentle hand on Emmeline's arm.

"Don't worry, Em. Maybe he'll forget your name."

"Don't be stupid!" said Emmeline, shaking her arm free. "How can he? When it's his own name too?"

This was very snappish for that usually placid, patient girl. But who could blame her? Thanks to the headlong methods of Jeannie's sister—of the Top-flight Fully-automated Junior High School Girl Detective—the investigation seemed only to be getting Emmeline's family deeper into the trouble from which it was supposed to be rescuing them.

14
A Disturbing Call

One more shock awaited Alison that day—though it was not altogether unpleasant.

It happened during the evening meal.

The whole family was present. They were having hamburgers and french fries. This was a great favorite with the girls, and whatever the clash with Mr. Lawrence S. Grant had done to Emmeline's appetite, it had made no difference to Alison's and Jeannie's. They were ravenous.

"Jeannie," said Mr. McNair, "I wish you would not take extra bites when your mouth is already full."

"Suwuff, Duffuff," she replied, rolling her eyes above the working jaws.

"That means, 'Sorry, Daddy,'" explained Alison. She turned to her sister. "And *I* wish you wouldn't talk with your mouth full."

"Yours isn't exactly empty," said Tom.

"No, but at least I've learned how to push the food into my cheek while I talk. You spit crumbs!"

117

"I do *not!*" said Tom, flushing.

"There, you did it then!" retorted Alison, pausing in her chewing.

"Yeauff!" agreed Jeannie, with a firm nod.

"Impossible!" muttered Mr. McNair. "Then they wonder why we don't take them out more often to eat with us. All three could use a few lessons in— why, what's the matter, dear?"

His wife hadn't been listening. She probably hadn't even heard the argument that preceded Mr. McNair's comments. Her own hamburger was scarcely touched. Her french fries were pushed to one side.

"Mm?"

"Come on, something's worrying you, isn't it?"

"Oh, it's nothing . . . I guess."

Mr. McNair pushed back his own plate.

"If you're not eating, I'm not eating."

"Can *I* have your french fries, Daddy?" asked Jeannie, her mouth empty for the moment.

"Finish your own, first," said Mrs. McNair. "Then you can have some of mine. . . . Oh, it's nothing, John," she said, turning to her husband. "Really."

Mr. McNair's eyes flashed.

"Well, in that case it won't hurt to tell us then, will it?"

Alison wasn't paying much attention to this, despite the sharp note in her father's voice. She had troubles of her own. The only interest the exchange had aroused so far was in the fate of her mother's french fries. She was darned if Jeannie was going to grab the lot.

But at her mother's next words Alison's rate of chewing began to fall off sharply.

"Oh well, if you insist!" Mrs. McNair was saying irritably. "I think I'm starting to get another round of obscene phone calls."

This brought Tom's jaws to a standstill. Only Jeannie continued lustily champing, as if nothing had happened.

Mr. McNair glanced uneasily at his children.

"Are you sure?"

"I think so. This time it's a man—"

"Aren't they always?"

"Let me finish, John, please. . . . This time it's a man with a throaty *confidential* type of voice. I mean as soon as I answered, he said—"

"Do you think the girls ought to hear this?"

"You did insist, you know! . . . Anyway, it was nothing bad in itself. But it was obviously a sort of preface to something bad, if you see what I mean."

Now Alison had stopped chewing. Tom remained immobile, with a piece of bun halfway to his mouth. Even Jeannie had slowed down. She seemed to be listening with widened eyes as well as her ears.

"Go on, then," said Mr. McNair.

He looked as if he wished he'd never started it.

"He said, in this hoarse, this *insinuating* voice, slightly Irish, I thought—he said: *'Hello, is that you, Kathleen, me darlint, me queen? I got something you'll be delighted to hear—'* And then of course I hung up. . . . What's the matter, Jeannie?"

The younger girl's eyes were rolling in agony as she made muffled protesting sounds through the hand clamped over her mouth.

It was Alison's hand: her left.

With her right hand she was busy slapping her sister's back.

"She started choking," said Alison.

This wasn't strictly correct. At the mention of "Irish" Jeannie's jaws had dropped open. At the mention of "Kathleen" she'd begun to speak. Already she'd uttered the words, "Why, that must have been—"

But, thanks to the habit she'd just been told off for, they came out as, "Wug! Thush mudder bee—" and to ears other than her sister's it really did sound like the beginning of a coughing fit.

"Excuse us," said Alison. "I think I'll take her to the bathroom. . . . All right now, honey?"

Jeannie nodded vigorously.

Alison took the hand from her mouth.

"Come on then. You'll feel better when you've rinsed your mouth out."

"Now that," said Mr. McNair, as they left the table, "is what I like to see. Alison looking after her kid sister. And even taking time off from her own eating to do it!"

"Thank you, Daddy," said Alison, in a gentle good-girl voice, from the doorway. Then she gave her kid sister a shove, closed the door, and growled ferociously: "You dummy! On no account do you tell them who that was! Hear? A good detective *never* betrays his sources of information, *ever!*"

"Sorry, Ally! It just started coming out when I realized who— Hey! I wonder what information he did have, though?"

"That's what I've been wondering," said Alison, in a calmer voice. "It must be something good, for him to spend a dime on a call. . . . Listen, you go to the bathroom and splash around while I call Emmeline from Mom and Dad's bedroom. The news will cheer her up."

But Emmeline's hopes had suffered too much that day to be raised so easily.

"Did you hear what I said, Em? *Mr. O'Connor has some vital information for us.* Now I know we can't go out looking for him right away, now that it's dark and all, they'd never let us. And I doubt if he'll risk another dime, after the reception he got from Mom. But we'll be sure to find him tomorrow—he's never far away—and he can tell us then. Don't forget —he said we'd be delighted to hear it, so it *must* be really good. . . . Emmeline—are you there?"

121

"Yes, I'm here, Ally."

The voice was small and sad.

Alison gave the phone an impatient shake.

"Well, what's with you then? Didn't you hear what I said? Is this a bad line?"

"No . . ." A sigh. "I heard you all right."

"Well then, don't you think it's great? What *is* the matter with you, Emmeline Grant?"

"I—I'm sorry, Ally. It's just that—well—Daddy came home tonight with another eighteen items on the list. *Eighteen,* Ally! And the slips from Macy's and other really big stores still haven't come in!"

That night, as she lay in bed, Alison decided that she couldn't really blame Emmeline for losing faith like that. After all, her friend had the most to lose. But the news that Mr. O'Connor might have a hot tip-off for them had revived all Alison's hopes, and she was more determined than ever to crack the case.

Even now, she thought—even before they got to know the exact details of this new information—there was a lot that could be done, if you just concentrated. True, it was a bewildering case. Sometimes it seemed as if they had too many details. And, like that day they watched the TV episode being shot, many of those details seemed crazy at first.

She smiled as she thought of the "cops" in denim shorts. When you got right down to it, they weren't even actors really. They were stunt-drivers. That was their true profession.

But as that afternoon had worn on, and the closer they'd watched, the more the girls had been able to understand what was really happening. It was just a matter of sticking with it. Concentrating. Watching every move.

"Yes—but where did *that* get us?"

Alison frowned. She could just imagine Emmeline saying those words in her present mood.

Then she shook her head briskly, dismissing such attitudes.

"Think positive!" she told herself. "Hang on in! Don't be put off by a bit of a blunder like today's. After all, it very easily *might* have been the perpetrator. If we'd heard the man being called 'Mr. Grant' and done nothing about it, we'd never have known for sure, would we?"

"Nyaow!" a voice replied in the darkness, startling her.

But it was only Norton. She felt the jolt of the bed as he jumped up, to settle down at her feet.

"So the word is *Think,* Norton, right? . . . Right! Think, think, think . . . Like for instance the facts we already know. What are they? I'll tell you. We know it's not a kid, for a start. Minors aren't allowed to have credit cards. O.K. So what else? Why, we know it has to be a *man,* don't we? That's because the card belongs to a man. It has Mr. Grant's name on it. A woman perpetrator might get away with it once or twice without being challenged. But not all those times. No way!"

Then immediately she had a new idea.

"Of course!" she said, sitting up with a jerk that had Norton rearing and staring at her with eyes that gleamed from the shadows. "Why didn't we think of this before?"

She was thinking of one of the few unvisited places

on the original list. The only nearby store they'd not inquired at.

She hadn't forgotten it. She'd deliberately been leaving it to the end, hoping they'd track down the perpetrator—or a good description of him—long before they got around to *that* place.

But now that she'd had her new idea she could have kicked herself for not making that store the first on the list—absolute Number One priority.

A "boutique" it called itself. But not the usual kind. It was a dim, creepy-looking joint, about ten blocks away, a place where some of the kids liked to peer into on the way from school, and giggle at, and whisper about furtively, and dare each other to enter —though none of them ever did.

And the purchase? What was it again, exactly?

She closed her eyes and the words came up again, just as if she'd been reading them directly: *1 garter belt, red*.

"Just think of it, Norton! A man! Buying something like that! Why, they'll be *sure* to remember him!"

And now she could hardly wait for morning. So great was her eagerness that Norton—after half an hour of trying to accommodate himself to the sudden hollows, peaks, and ridges caused by her tossing and turning and kicking and twisting and stretching— jumped off the bed with a growl of disgust and demanded to be let out of the room.

15

Spiderella's Boutique

It's tough being a police detective in New York City. You have to go into so many sleazy places. Even girl cops have it to do—well, *especially* girl cops, if they're actually on the N.Y.P.D. payroll and are over twenty-one. But the same applies to schoolgirl detectives also, it seems, as Alison and the others found out. There could be no shirking it.

Not that Spiderella's Boutique was all that bad. Even Alison in her eagerness would have known better than to pursue her investigations right through the doors of and into a shady bar, say. But Spiderella's Boutique certainly *looked* pretty spooky.

It was located in a side street between Park and Lexington. It had two long, narrow display windows, one on either side of the doorway—windows that were little more than horizontal slits compared to normal store windows. And they were decorated with artificial cobwebs. Festoons and swags of nylon strands hung there behind tinted glass in a dim greenish light, and it was on these stands—like ladybugs and dragonflies caught in a web—that various articles of clothing were displayed: mostly night-gowns and pieces of underwear, all flimsy, all flashy.

It smelled pretty spooky, too. It smelled of a cheap and heavy perfume, and it was an odor that rolled to meet the girls halfway along the street, even as early as nine-fifteen in the morning. It was as if the owners gave the sidewalk outside the store a lavish spraying of the stuff every day, instead of the normal sweeping and swilling with plain hot water and deter-gent. It was so strong at the doorway that Alison checked in the middle of taking a deep breath that she'd started. To boost her courage, she made do with crossing her fingers instead.

"Come on," she muttered. "Let's get it over with."

Jeannie was too young to realize just how creepy the place was, so she followed her sister eagerly enough. But Emmeline's face was burning with a deep blush and it remained there right through to the end of the interview. Only Alison kept her face clear and her mind sharply concentrated on the one impor-tant thing: the investigation.

And, immediately, her courage and persistence were rewarded. It wasn't half as creepy inside as she'd imagined. There were more artificial cobwebs in various display cases and on stands, with more garish items of clothing seemingly caught up in them, but as yet the three girls were the only visitors and the young woman sitting behind the glass counter was surprisingly homely.

"Hi!" she said nonchalantly, not even bothering to look at them, being apparently more concerned with

126

a package of chewing gum in her hands. She selected three sticks and added them to the wad that was already bulging her cheeks. "Breakfash!" she explained, in a voice that was uncannily like Jeannie's at mealtimes. "C'n I do forya?"

She was very fat. Her clothes were nondescript: a shapeless black sweater, sprinkled with dandruff, and old blue slacks. Her complexion was mealy and she was completely without make-up, save for the turquoise eye shadow she'd daubed above and below two sets of enormous false lashes.

"Excuse me?" said Alison, who'd recognized the word "breakfast" but hadn't been able to make out the rest.

The woman thrust the gum to the side of her mouth. Still without looking at them, looking instead at the stack of perfume bottles on the counter, at the side of a card that read: ONE WHIFF AND HE'S YOURS —*The Perfume He'll Find Irresistible*—she said:

"What—can—I—do—for—you?"

"Oh, sure—sorry!" said Alison, rather disarmed by the gentle way the woman had emphasized her words, without a trace of sarcasm. "Well, you see . . ."

And so she embarked on her story.

The woman listened patiently, with dipped head, nodding from time to time, and occasionally giving her wad of gum a blow and a crack to show she was still with them. But at the end of it all she shook her head and the huge lashes fluttered and she gave the girls one of her rare direct looks.

"Sorry, kids. Can't help ya there. Nergh . . ." She

shook her head again and gave the gum a very positive snap. "See, duringa day, place is crowded. Truly. Not like now. Couldn't remember from all those faces. Besides," she lowered her voice and gave them another quick glance, "we're not suppose to stare at them too much. Accounta embarrassing them."

Emmeline nodded, her lips tight between the blazing cheeks. She looked as if she could well understand that, having just been glancing around at some of the displays.

Alison wasn't so easily deterred, however.

"But surely if a *man* came in and bought a garter belt, it would be so unusual that—"

She broke off, arrested by a giant explosion of the gum. The woman laughed.

"Baby!" she said. "Men are our best customers! Birthday gifts for their wives and girl friends. Specially around three and four inna afternoon, for some reason. And not just fellas either—ner! Li'l old ladies, 'n girls you'd think was only innerested in cooking organic food 'n doing macramé work 'n stuff like that. Why, it's only—"

Then she too had to break off.

This was because a man had walked in from the back and was making gasping croaking noises at her.

"Hey! hey! hey!"

The three girl visitors bunched a little closer. Even Jeannie seemed a little scared now, as she tightened her grip on the sling of her weighted purse.

For the newcomer was like nothing so much as a huge toad—squat and ugly and dressed in what looked like green velvet. Even his skin had a greenish cast in that light.

128

"These kids friends of yours, Toni?"

"Nuh-huh! They just stopped by to—"

"Well, get rid of them! Caincha see they're minors?"

The woman gave Alison a friendly nod.

"That's what I was juss gonna say. It's only minors we don't do business with in here."

"Toni! Ya hear what I said?"

The young woman sighed and gave her gum another crack. This time it had a definitely insolent ring to it. Then she shrugged and turned to the girls:

"You heard what the—uh—gemmun said, kids. Sorry I wasn't able to help. Have a good day now."

Alison hesitated. The toad man was on his way back to whatever stone he'd come from under. She accepted what the woman had said, but now that the main investigation had drawn a blank, she allowed her attention to wander a little—over to a small private mystery concerning Greg Peters and what on earth it was he could see in Nan Stafford.

"By the way," she said. "About this perfume here —" She nodded toward the stack of bottles and the card. "Has a girl a bit older than me, with mousy hair, cold blue eyes, and thick ankles ever—?"

"Out!" cried the toad man, spinning around and looking ready to jump. "Out! Out! Out!"

They nearly tripped over one another in their rush to hit the street. And even there they didn't slow down until they were out of nose-shot of the perfume.

Then, immediately, a deep gloom fell over them.

"Too bad!" murmured Alison. "I'd really been counting on that."

"I feel as if I'll never get rid of the smell until I've showered and changed all my clothes!" said Emmeline.

"I'd have zonked him with my purse!" said Jeannie.

"Forget *him!*" snapped Alison. "Forget the *smell!* We're on an investigation, remember?"

"Huh! Tell me about it!" grunted Emmeline. "The only thing about your *investigation* is we never find anything that might even *start* to help us track down the card."

"Oh no, Emmeline Grant? Well, just you listen to—"

Alison's retort was cut short by a friendly bellow.

"So *there* y'are, me darlings! I been lookin' all over town for yez!"

It was Mr. O'Connor, rearing up in front of them with the shiny swagger-stick held like a wand: a shabby, ragged Fairy Godfather.

Their despondency fled, as if by magic.

"Gosh! Mr. O'Connor! Was that you who—?"

"Kathleen, you must have gave me the wrong number," he said reproachfully. "When I called it I do believe it was the Women's Jail at Riker's Island that I got, with the head lady warden herself answering, she sounded so chilly. Brrr! But anyways—here y'all are now, and here's yer old pal with a real hot tip-off for yez."

"Oh, Mr. O'Connor! Honestly?"

"Of *course* honestly, Adeline! Would I be foolin' when there's real money at stake? Eh, Kathleen? . . . No. Listen. I think I got a real good description of the guy you're looking for. And that's the truth!"

16
Corky's Evidence

All around the three girls and the man the city went about its business. Taxis hooted, trucks rattled by, vacuum brakes hissed, gears were changed with a grinding of monstrous metal teeth, a motorbike rasped, a siren wailed, another siren made a piping, warbling sound, a helicopter chattered overhead, and vague rumblings came from under their feet, where the IRT Lexington subway ran.

But although the girls could hear all this noise, none of it really registered. They might just as well have been standing at a corner of Main Street in some little country town. Or at the side of a desert highway.

They were entranced. They had ears only for the words of the dusty gray figure that loomed over them, accenting his syllables with curious little stabs and twirls of the polished wand.

". . . and who should I run into but this old buddy of mine, Corky Riley, a fine man but terribly cursed with bad luck one way or the other, nothing ever going right for him. Fact, he's so unlucky he's developed this sixth sense which tells him in advance where trouble might be lurking, so that he's always changing his mind and his plans and even his direction, when going from one place to another. It's the truth I'm telling you when I say that sometimes it takes Corky over an hour to walk five blocks because of the detours his sixth sense keeps telling him to make. And that was the way of it on the afternoon we're all interested in."

"Monday last week?" said Alison, almost breathless in her anxiety that Mr. O'Connor hadn't made a mistake.

"On the Monday afternoon of last week. At between five and five-thirty, isn't that what you said? . . . Right. So let me tell you. Along the right street at the right time came the right man, me old friend Corky Riley, taking a message from a gentleman in Donnelly's Bar over on First Avenue to another gentleman who is a janitor in a building on Third Avenue—which shows you just how far his sixth sense had taken him out of his way that afternoon, though of course it was very lucky for us that it did."

"But are you sure—?"

"Those were me very own words, Adeline, me love. 'Now are ye sure, Corky,' I said, 'that you was in the particular street I'm talking about, between Park and Madison, at that time?' And Corky glares up at me through them thick pebble glasses he wears and he says, 'Am I ever likely to forget it? That old sixth sense of mine nearly had a nervous breakdown coping with the hazards in that terrible street, and I swear to you, Kevin, I'll never pass through it again. It's a minefield of misfortunes for a man as afflicted as meself.' "

"Poor man! I hope—"

"Shut up, Jeannie! Go on, Mr. O'Connor. What hazards was he talking about?"

"Again my very own words, Kathleen. 'What hazards would they be, Corky?' I says. 'I'll tell you,' says he, and he holds up one finger. 'The first is a fool of a youth, a great gangling gossoon, with a pack of dogs, some of them the size of donkeys. At rush hour, mark you, and them prancing around on the ends of leashes causing honest elderly citizens to play at jump rope against their inclinations. That was Hazard Number One.' "

"That was Rollo!"

"Jeannie! Go on, Mr. O'Connor, please."

"So then Corky holds up another finger and he says, 'Hazard Number Two nearly gave me heart failure just to see it, Kevin. Because as true as I stand here I thought for a minute it was one of them bushes from the center of Park Avenue that had grown legs and was taking a walk.' "

"Excuse me, Mr.—uh—Kevin. This Corky. He hadn't been drinking, had he?"

"Not a drop, darling. He took the pledge years ago, when he found that liquor fogged up his sixth sense and was doubling and trebling his bad luck. No, he was as sober as a judge, though I must say I was beginning to wonder about the state of his mind, all this talk of bushes walking. But he soon explained

133

it. 'It wasn't a bush of course, but it was just as bad, being a huge great bunch of flowers some little eejut of a fella was carrying in front of his puss so he couldn't possibly see where he was going. And you know what?' says Corky. 'That guy would have blundered straight into me and knocked me into the traffic, I could see it coming, if he hadn't blundered into Hazard Number One and his thundering dogs first.' "

"Was he talking about your father, Emmeline? Because—"

"Hush, honey!"

"Well, I wouldn't let him call *my* daddy an idiot!"

"That's just Corky's way of talking, Janet, me pet. The poor guy's so scared of running into trouble he hardly knows what he's saying at times. Anyway, where was I?"

"Where Mr. Grant got tangled with Rollo's dogs."

"Ah, yes, Kathleen. Thank you. Hazards Number One and Two. So then it was the *main* one. The main one as far as *we're* concerned, anyway. 'And Hazard Number Three,' says Corky, sticking up another finger, 'was lying in wait for me just across the street.' *'Lying in wait,* Corky?' says I. 'Well, *crouching* in wait then,' says he—and of course that's when I really pricked up my ears. 'Tell me about it, Corky,' I said. 'That's what I'm trying to do, man!' he replied. 'I mean tell me what this person was doing, and what he or she looked like. Exactly.' 'Well, *exactly* I can't be sure of,' he says, 'because as soon as I see him I decide to have no dealings with that side of the street at all, on account that if *I* don't trip over the fool, someone else will, and fall in front of me, and bring me down too, and then I'd be sure to break an arm at least. So I take a chance on Hazards Four through Five Million, which is the New York traffic, and step off the sidewalk and skirt around the guys with the dogs and the flowers, and I'm lucky, save that a patrol car had to brake pretty quick and the cop inside said he'd half a mind to give me a ticket for jaywalking again.' "

Mr. O'Connor stopped to grin.

"That Corky!" he said. "All the cops know him."

"But the stooping figure, Mr. O'Connor. Did he say—?"

"He did, he did! What this guy was doing, Corky said, was either tying his shoestring or picking something up. And what he looked like—well—I got to admit that Corky is a bit nearsighted. It's the main cause of his bad luck, I always think. But don't look so disappointed, Kathleen. *This* guy even Corky couldn't give a bad description of, even from across the street. I mean the way he was dressed, this guy, it was unmistakable. 'He had on a long black gown,' says Corky, 'down to his ankles. And he also had on one of them little hats, like short-order cooks wear, only black, not white. It was some kind of priest.' "

Mr. O'Connor's yellow-gray face split open in a grin of triumph to reveal a row of crooked yellow teeth. He gave his baton a twirl.

"How's about *that* for a clear description, huh?"

Alison nodded rapidly.

"They call those hats birettas," she said. "Pretty unusual." Her breathing was coming quick. "But what else? Was he old? Bearded? Young? Black? Caucasian?"

The man's grin widened.

"Clean-shaven. Caucasian. Corky was positive about that, too. The face was only a blur to him at that range, but Corky's not color-blind and he said yes. This was a white guy. 'Pink' was the word he used. And right away that reminded me. There has been one strolling around here these past few days. Just a kid, he looks. Wandering around with a dumb, peaceful smile on his puss."

Alison frowned.

"But someone like that wouldn't keep the card and —and use it illegally."

"Heh! Bless yer innocent heart, Kathleen! Of course he wouldn't. If he was genu-wine. But in this jungle, who knows? That could be the perfect disguise for some jerk who earns his bread passing phony credit cards."

Alison was nodding. Her eyes were bright as she fumbled in her purse. Everything seemed to be clicking into place at last. And with a wonderful description like that, how could they go wrong? Even in the world's busiest streets a young priest with an unusual black hat shouldn't be so hard to track down, if he continued to operate in the same area.

"That's worth a whole dollar to begin with, Mr. O'Connor!" she said. "And many thanks."

He crumpled it into a ball and sent it rolling silently into the depths of his pocket.

"I was hoping ye'd think so, Kathleen, me sweet. I've got rather a heavy federal tax bill this year and me cash-flow's turning into a trickle. . . . Tell me, though, seriously. D'je get any more leads?"

"None as good as *that*," said Emmeline, flushing again, but this time with excitement.

"She's right!" said Alison, magnanimous in her own excitement. "Apart from the facts that it's a man, and all the stores he's used it in so far are in Manhattan, and that most of them are not far from here."

"Ah, but that's good, very good! It shows that he's a beginner in spite of his clever disguise. A real pro would have taken it to another city to use, or another part of town. That's if he didn't take it and sell it over the river, like I told you he might. And if it *is* a beginner, he's bound to slip up sooner or later."

Emmeline's face clouded.

"Yes. But it better be sooner," she said. "Later's no good. Any later than Friday is *too* late."

This reminded Alison that there was still work to be done.

"But now you've given us this marvelous tip-off, Mr. O'Connor, we can really build up a profile of the perpetrator. . . . Come on, you two. So long, Kevin—and thanks again."

Their informant gave them a cheery wave.

"I'll keep in touch!" he called after them.

"What's a profile?" said Jeannie.

"It's when you gather all the details known about a perpetrator," said Alison. "And you fit them together. And a picture of him emerges. We'll go right back to my—to the squad room—and get to work on it."

But Emmeline stopped in her tracks and caused

the other two to turn back. The plump girl's look of excitement was still there in her eyes, but now it was reinforced with a stubborn gleam that Alison knew well.

"What is it now?" she said.

"I appreciate your enthusiasm, Ally," Emmeline replied. "And I can see what you mean about profiles and things. But there *are* only two or three days left. And it *is* my father's job that's at stake."

"So?"

"So I say we waste no more time on theories and get looking for that phony priest. At least we can check with some of the stores again, now that we have such a vivid description to give them."

"Yeah!" said Jeannie. "That squad-room stuff, that blackboard and chalk and maps and pins—it—*it's like school!*"

Alison shrugged.

Rebellion among her followers she could normally handle. But it *was* Emmeline who had most to lose, she had to admit. What was more, her friend was probably right. For once.

"O.K.," she said. "But we'll do it my way or not at all."

"Which is *what?*" said Emmeline, still with a determined glint in her eyes.

"Methodically. Scientifically. Working through the list again."

"Oh, that!" said Emmeline. "Sure, Ally. Just lead the way."

17
The Figure in the Long Black Robe

And so—methodically, scientifically, working their way through the list again—they started making the rounds of all the stores they had visited previously.

They were sustained in this task by two things. First the fact, already pointed out by Emmeline, that they now had a vivid description to give to the store clerks. And second the even more stimulating fact, pointed out by Alison between the first two rechecks, that:

"We never know when we might bump into him while we're making our visits. I've got a funny feeling he's around here someplace, that it's just a matter of time before our paths cross. And now we know what he looks like—well! Keep your eyes open, girls, and we have him cold!"

It was perhaps a good thing that they did have this second possibility in mind, otherwise they would probably have lost heart again long before they did.

Because in the stores it was the same old story over again. The only difference was that most of the clerks grew even more irritable. The following was a typical exchange:

"I thought I told you kids yesterday that—"

"Yes, sir. We know. And we appreciate your interest, remembering us."

"Yeah, well, who could forget?"

"But today we have a clearer picture ourselves of the man who bought the silver cigarette lighter. He had a long black robe and a little black hat and—"

"Say, what *is* this? Now I *know* you're fooling! If you don't get outa my hair, right now, I'll call a cop. I mean it."

"But, sir, really—we're serious. Don't you recall a priest, young, Caucasian—"

"No, I don't! Now leave. Get out. And don't come back!"

The man who'd sold the perpetrator a watch was one of the very few who listened with intelligent respect.

"You *sure* it was a guy like that picked up the card?"

"Pretty sure, yes, sir. Almost definitely. We had very reliable information."

"We sure did! It cost us a dollar!"

"Be quiet, Jeannie . . . sir?"

"Hmm, well . . . let's suppose it was one hundred per cent correct, and this was some sort of phony outfit he was wearing at the time. What makes you think he wouldn't change into ordinary clothes when he goes shopping around with the card? Huh? I mean, sure—if a guy dressed like that *had* been in and bought the watch, I'd have remembered. But isn't that just what he wants to avoid?"

"You mean—?"

"I mean, honey, that there's disguises and disguises. In a crowded street, for someone who's a pickpocket, say, the priest outfit is perfect. Nobody suspects one of them of being crooked. And so, *out there,* nobody gives him a second glance. But in a store, when a guy actually buys something, and speaks to you, and waits around for his sales slip and his card back—well then there's enough time for his outfit to register in the clerk's mind. I mean it's not every day a priest with a hat like that walks in—especially a young one. Right?"

Sadly, the girls had to agree.

This visit occurred toward the end of the afternoon, and there were still a half-dozen stores left on the list—but the man's words took most of the heart out of the investigators.

"Well, Emmeline," said Alison, out in the street, "it was your idea, and it was a good one. But the more I think about what the man said, the more I have to agree that it makes sense."

"I guess so," murmured Emmeline, all the earlier fight gone.

"We still might bump into him in the street, though!" said Jeannie, game to the end, swinging her purse and looking around eagerly.

"*If* he's in his priest outfit, yes," said Alison. "But

if he's just shopping—well—" She shrugged. "In his ordinary clothes we could have brushed past him already and never known it."

Emmeline shivered.

"It's getting cold. And I'm hungry. Can we—uh—shall we call it a day?"

"Suits me," said Alison. "But don't worry, Em. You take a good rest tonight and you'll feel all the fresher when we resume our investigations tomorrow morning. Meanwhile, I'll attack the case from another angle."

"What other angle?"

"The one I mentioned this morning, which you were both so quick to shoot down." Alison sounded rather smug, despite the fact that she did her best to conceal it. "The profile angle. This evening I'm going to sift through all the details we've got so far and I'm going to build up a picture of the perpetrator that will be good and vivid whether he's in his priest outfit or not. You'll see."

She was as good as her word. In fact she built up more than one good and vivid picture of the perpetrator. The only trouble was that most of them were rather *too* vivid.

The first was pure fantasy. It leaped into her mind right after supper, even as she assumed her best thinking position. (Face down, stretched out on the bed, with her knees bent and her feet in the air, gently dandling the slippers at the end of her thoughtfully wriggling toes.)

This was a picture of a tall, sinister figure in a

billowing robe, crouching at the edge of a river at sundown. He was busy tossing ping-pong balls into the water, muttering strange Latin words as he did so. Then he suddenly straightened up, looked at the brand-new watch on his wrist, and drew from the folds of his robe a huge, pearly-gray ram's horn. He put it to his lips, leaned back and, silhouetted like that against the blood-red glare of the setting sun, blew three deep but penetrating blasts on the horn. This had the effect of making the black water seethe between the bobbing ping-pong balls, and that was the signal for him to start fishing. But instead of a pole, he simply held the lines between his fingers, like Rollo with the dog leashes. There were at least eight of them, with the artificial flies at the ends of them glittering in the last rays of the sun like sparks. Then—

But here Alison shook her head briskly and impatiently. This was getting her nowhere. It was the sort of picture she might have accepted and gone to work on in her witchcraft days, but not now.

"A detective has to be practical and objective at all times!" she said, to no one in particular. (Because Jeannie had flatly refused to participate in what she continued to call "dumb schoolroom stuff," and was sitting watching television in the living room, with Norton on her lap.) "Scientific," added Alison. "Thinking about probabilities—not wild, impossible stuff like that!"

So saying, she reached to the bedside table and ran her practical, objective eyes down along the list of purchases again.

Then she really began to build her profiles, even though it was a negative aspect that struck her first.

"One thing we can rule out," she murmured thoughtfully, "is identifying him at a glance from some article of clothing on the list."

What she meant was that it contained no eye-catching, wide-brimmed straw hat, like the one the kidnaper had worn in the television episode; or a fancy pair of shoes or boots; or even a loud necktie with a distinctive pattern. For a second or two, a grin spread across her face as she thought of the red garter belt and imagined the priest wearing it outside his robe. But that was fantasizing again, and she gave her head another brisk shake to stop it. The garter belt was obviously for some girl friend, and as a means of quick identification the investigators might as well forget it.

But there were other kinds of pictures besides straight *appearances,* she told herself, with a grave nod of the head.

"Like for instance," she said, frowning at an imaginary questioner, "pictures of a person's tastes and habits. Now them we *can* build up from the list. . . ."

She reached for her notebook and pen. She closed her eyes for a moment, while she thought of a suitable heading. Then she began:

Profile #1: The Perpetrator as a Sportsman

That was obvious. He was a keen fisherman, wasn't he? Why else buy those expensive, very special flies?

She nodded in answer and wrote down:

> *Keen fisherman—purchase of artificial flies.*

Then there were the ping-pong balls. Two dozen, he'd bought. Dismissing the dream picture of the scene by the river that she'd conjured up earlier, Alison could see quite clearly only one possible practical reason for their purchase. She wrote:

> *Keen table-tennis player. Practices a lot. Probably has terrific smash shot and needs lots of replacements.*

She glanced over the list again, seeking further evidence of sporting activities. Eventually she shook her head and was about to start on a different track, when she remembered the wallet.

"Penn Station!" she said. "Of course!"

It hadn't been the trains he'd gone down there for, or even Macy's just around the corner. Jeannie had come closest, after all—though it wasn't the circus either.

> *Probably a hockey fan* (she scribbled). *Or basketball. See visit to Penn Station and check on games at Madison Square Garden that date.*

Having decided she'd squeezed all she could out of the list to fit into her first profile, she turned the page and wrote down her next heading.

> *Profile #2: The Perpetrator as Artist*

This began quite strongly with a couple of items from the list: a set of assorted poster paints in jars and, purchased at the same store at the same time, three camel-hair brushes of different sizes.

"The brushes alone, sure," Alison said to another imaginary (and rather dumb) questioner (she had Emmeline in mind). "He could have bought the brushes to apply oil to some machinery with. Or to clean out a typewriter . . . But the poster paint leaves us in no doubt. No doubt *at all*. He's a keen amateur artist. Has to be."

But that was that for the profile as well as the argument. After starting out so promisingly, Alison was rather miffed to find no other purchase that could be made to fit in this case.

She went on to the next.

Profile ✗3: The Perpetrator as Music Lover

This turned out to be as fruitful as the first one.

As early as the previous Wednesday, the man had gone and bought himself a complete set of records, boxed, of Beethoven's Late Quartets.

"Just like he couldn't wait, like he'd been wanting them for *ages!*" said Alison. "And the reason I say that is down here, see." She tapped the list. "He even got them before he bought this."

She was tapping the item: *1 portable record player, $85 plus tax.*

"That was Friday, note. Hey—and that gives us another bit of valuable information! Since he's obviously such a keen music lover, how come he hadn't got a record player already? I'll tell you why. *Be-cause he's only just come from someplace where they're not allowed to have them!*"

Scribbling wildly, she wrote:

Perpetrator just released from jail.

Then, as she read it over, even her bold nerve failed, and she changed the period to a query.

But it was a strong possibility, nobody could deny that!

Finally, returning to the list, she selected the ram's horn, bought by the perpetrator in a store special-izing in decorative shells, and included it in the profile.

"He *could* have bought it for prettying up his room, I suppose. But my guess is that he's a student of ancient instruments and he couldn't resist buying this to experiment with."

That last theory did seem to stretch the facts a bit, but by then Alison's mind had started grappling with the problem of how to use the three profiles to the best advantage. . . .

"But I don't *get* it, Alison!" Emmeline said, the next morning, as they left the Grant apartment.

"Me either!" grumbled Jeannie.

"I mean how can this—this stuff"—Emmeline looked up from Alison's notebook and handed it back with a sniff—"how can it possibly help us to identify the man quickly enough?"

"Easy!" said Alison. "Because if he *is* a keen stu-dent of old musical instruments, he probably goes to the Metropolitan Museum or some place like that every day. Where they have rooms full of the things. We'll ask Rollo, he'll know. And we'll stake the place out."

Emmeline groaned.

"I tell you there isn't *time*. If we were real police detectives—"

"Yes. That's another thing," said Alison. "I admit this next idea isn't much good to *us,* but if I was a police lieutenant like that dumbbell on TV, I'd have someone checking into the records of all recent prison releases right away."

"Big deal!" said Jeannie. "Hey! We gonna stand around here all day? All we have to do is look for a man in a long black robe and a little black hat. Isn't that good enough to be working on?"

Alison gave her sister her most withering "poor simple kid" smile. Then she turned back to Emmeline.

"But of course I am *not* a real police lieutenant. I also admit that staking out the music rooms in museums *would* take time. And I'm not even suggesting attending the next hockey game at the Garden, though he *is,* quite obviously, a Rangers fan. Neither am I in any doubt about our manpower resources not being enough to check with all the Y's in town. You know—for information about first-class ping-pong players with terrific smash techniques—even though that would definitely help us to catch him before long. Oh no . . . my profiles have pointed me to a much better line of action."

They were now on the front step of the building.

Alison waited there, smiling from one puzzled face to the other.

"Go on, then," said Emmeline, half irritable, half eager. "What?"

"Well take the Artist Profile first. What do we find? We find he bought the paints and the brushes at the same time, right?"

"Yes. Right. But—"

"Moving on to the Music Profile, we find another pair of items that go together—the records and the record player. O.K.? . . . Save that this time he bought them on two separate occasions. See?"

"Yes, yes." Emmeline winced a little as she nodded. Next to a Japanese twelve-inch portable TV set, price $89.99, the record player had been the man's most expensive purchase. "Using my father's card to do it with," she added, probably hoping to remind her friend that this was no game. "Oh, come on, Ally —what are you getting at?"

Alison was unruffled, unhurried. She continued:

"Now, flipping back to the Sports Profile, what do we find there?"

Emmeline glowered at the notes.

"Well, no matching items, if that's what you mean."

Alison smiled broadly.

"No. Not *yet*. But remember how we thought he might be following up his fishing-flies purchase by buying a rod?"

Emmeline shuddered.

"We do not go *there* again!" she said. "No matter what!"

"I'm not talking about there," said Alison. "I'm talking about this other sporting-goods store. On Madison. Where he got the box of ping-pong balls. My hunch is that he's such a keen player it won't be long before he goes back to buy a pair of championship standard paddles."

She closed her book, glowing with triumph.

Emmeline still looked doubtful.

"I see what you mean, Ally. But it's an awfully long shot."

"It's the best we've got," said Alison simply. Then she became brisk again. "So let's give it a spin. Now."

Jeannie giggled as they hurried along to the corner of Madison.

"What's with *you?*" said Alison.

"Your joke."

"What joke?"

"About giving it a spin."

"What's so funny about that?"

"Well, ping-pong balls. That's what you do to them, isn't it? Give them a spin?"

She giggled again.

Emmeline sighed. Alison rolled her eyes and groaned.

"My sister the comic!" she said. "Jeannie—just be quiet, huh? You might need your breath for running if we do spot him. All right?"

"Give it a spin!" said Jeannie again. "Heh! heh!"

She was still giggling three blocks farther down Madison, when suddenly she stopped and began to choke and flap her arms about.

"There!" said Alison. "That's with walking fast and laughing at the same time!"

She moved to give her sister's back a sharp slap, but Jeannie swerved, still flapping her hand.

"Nuh-oh!" she coughed. "I—uh—*along there!*"

Now the other two saw that the flapping hand was indicating something down the side street they'd just arrived at.

"*What* along there?"

"Huh-huh-*him!*"

Jeannie began to move down the street, still tottering a little as she coughed.

"Him?"

"Yeah! The—the phony priest! The per- perforator! The man in the robe and the funny black hat!"

Without slackening their pace, they stared ahead. The sidewalk was fairly crowded, even in that side street, even at that time of the day, and at first they thought she'd been imagining things.

Then Alison gasped as, out from the throng and across the street between the stalled traffic, there strode a tall figure in a black biretta and long, swirling, black robe.

18
Waiting to Pounce

There was no doubt in their minds now that this was the man mentioned by their informant.

"What now?" said Emmeline, as they crossed the street after him.

"We follow him," said Alison. "We see exactly where he goes and what he does."

"Like we did with the fishing-pole man," said Jeannie, speaking without a trace of irony but with a great deal of smugness.

"I hope it doesn't *end* like that!" said Emmeline.

"You're talking too much, both of you," said Alison. "Just keep quiet and don't lose sight of him, that's all."

"Who *spotted* him, huh?" said Jeannie.

Alison didn't answer.

It was not that their quarry required great concentration. Now that they were onto him, he was a much easier person to shadow than Mr. Lawrence Grant had been. Apart from his very distinctive clothing, his height helped a lot, with the black hat bobbing way above the heads and shoulders of most of the passers-by. Then again there was his pace: nice, firm, even strides, but not too fast.

"He *looks* genuine," said Emmeline at one point, after they'd been tailing him for five or six blocks.

Alison grunted.

She knew what her friend meant. The young man seemed to have his mind fixed on far higher things than the city streets. He walked with his head well up, never turning it from side to side. She couldn't see his eyes, of course, but from the way he was holding his head she guessed those eyes would be fixed steadily, absent-mindedly, above the heads of the people around him, meditating.

But that was part of the pose. It stood to reason. Anybody who took the trouble to dress like that wouldn't make the mistake of going around furtively, half crouched, stopping and starting and darting crafty glances from side to side, like some television crook.

"What do you *expect* him to look like?" she snapped at her friend. "Want he should be wearing a mask and flashing a switchblade?"

She spoke more sharply than she might have done because she herself had begun to suffer a series of disappointments.

For instance, they had already passed two art dealers on Madison, their windows ablaze with colorful paintings, and the man hadn't turned his head for so much as a brief passing glance. Thus had he torpedoed her Artist Profile.

Then, in a side street, he had passed a young man with a beard who'd been sitting on a stoop playing a flute—quite brilliantly, too. But the "priest" had neither faltered in his stride nor inclined an ear. Thus had he silently sliced up her Music Profile, leaving it in shreds to be wafted with the flute's notes into the polluted air.

And now, even as she thought wistfully of all that wasted thinking the night before, they were entering another side street, where some boys were playing catch across the roofs of the passing cars, and the man wasn't giving them or their curving ball a glance either. In fact—she faltered in her own stride as she saw one of the boys miss his catch and the ball rebound from the wall of a building and fly past the man's chest, almost brushing it—in fact he didn't even begin to make a grab at it, as most people would. He just ignored it, walking on at that same steady pace, head in air. Thus did he destroy, without lifting a finger, her carefully built-up Sportsman Profile.

"But he *is* our man," said Alison, three blocks later. "I could swear to it."

"Huh?" said Jeannie.

"But he's *done* nothing!" said Emmeline.

"Yet!" said Alison firmly. "He's done nothing *yet*. But haven't you noticed something?"

"What?"

"We're almost back where we first saw him. Right? . . ."

The man turned the corner in front of them.

"And *there!*" said Alison, hurrying up. "How about *that?* It looks like he's starting to cover the exact same route all over again!"

This turned out to be correct. With the girls still following him, the man did go over the same route, at the same steady pace and in the same seemingly dreamy manner.

"He can't be just not *caring* where he walks," said Alison, on the second circuit. "There must be *some* purpose."

"Yes," said Emmeline. She had begun to look far more alert since they'd picked out this pattern in his movements. "He—he's certainly gotten something in mind. Must have."

"Why must he have?" grumbled Jeannie.

The more alert the other two became, the more bored she was getting. Jeannie was raring for action, for something to swing that weighted purse at—not patterns.

Alison ignored her.

"You bet he must have something in mind," she said to Emmeline. "And you can bet also that it's something crooked. He's waiting to pounce. I can feel it in my bones."

She uttered the last two sentences in such a grim tone that even Jeannie brightened up.

And she wasn't disappointed this time.

For *pounce* is exactly what the man did.

Alison's bones had never been more reliable.

It happened not long after she'd made her prophecy. They were in a part of the circuit between Third and Lexington avenues, in the busy fifties. It was a street made narrower by parked trucks and dumpers full of rubble, and noisier by the sounds of heavy excavating machinery behind a board fence. A little knot of idlers were standing near a gap in the boards, rubbernecking at the construction workers below, and it was just before he reached them that the priest suddenly checked his pace, coming almost to a stand-still.

This in itself was enough to make the girls stiffen up and catch one another by the arm, because it was the first time the man's even walking rhythm had been broken—apart from when the lights were against him at intersections.

"Now what?" murmured Alison.

"He—oh—*look!*" cried Emmeline.

The man had taken off, no longer relaxed, dreamy, head in air, but crouching, tense, and very fast, like a running back.

"Hey!"

The hoarse cry arose from one of the idlers. He'd been sipping from a bottle in a brown bag and had stepped back a pace into the priest's path. Then he'd been brushed aside like a drunken wasp.

"Why'n cha look where ya goin', sister?" he yelled, staring blearily after the figure in the long flowing robe.

Jeannie laughed at his mistake, but Alison and Emmeline hustled her along between them, too concerned for jokes. The thought had just crossed Alison's mind that the man might be giving them the slip.

Then once again the girls stopped abruptly.

And not just because the man himself had stopped abruptly.

They were pulled up short by the sheer frightening nature of what he was doing.

"Gosh!"

"Oh, Ally! What shall we *do?*"

A woman had been standing by the boards a little farther along: a middle-aged woman with blue-white hair and a sealskin jacket. She'd been looking in her purse, as if checking to see whether she'd forgotten her keys or something.

But that was before the man in the robe had pounced—grabbing her purse with one hand and one of her wrists with the other, then spinning her around and slamming her against the boards with a sickening thud.

The woman yelled. It was a strange, deep, baying sound—a mixture of pain, terror, and alarm.

"Oh!" moaned Emmeline, beginning to tremble.

Jeannie whimpered and clung to Alison's sleeve.

And Alison stood still, perfectly still, trying to quell her own trembling.

There was no question now of using their weighted purses to aid the woman. Shocked by the sight and sound of real violence, the girls suddenly realized how puny they were.

But then came another shock.

The woman jerked her head as she struggled with her face to the boards, and all at once her hair fell off.

"It—it's a wig!" whispered Emmeline.

Then:

"All *right* already!" said the woman, in harsh masculine tones. "Ya wanna break my arm, ya big jerk? What are ya, some kinda nut?"

The assailant didn't reply at first. He hitched the woman's purse up over his shoulder and, with the free hand this gave him, he plucked at the back of his robe. The black cloth lifted to reveal a pair of dark pants, a belt—and a pair of handcuffs. These he deftly unclipped and brought around in front of him to clamp over the wrist he'd been holding with such a fierce grip all this time.

Then he spoke.

"You have the right to remain silent—"

"Oh yeah?" The contorted wigless face twisted back to scowl at him. It was heavily made up, but by now the watchers could see that this was no woman. "So let's see some identification, *officer!*"

Again the big man dipped under his robe. This time the groping hand came back with a wallet.

He spun the prisoner around to face him and flipped the wallet open in front of "her" eyes.

"O.K.?" he said. "O.K. . . . You have the right to remain silent . . ."

The girls gaped, hardly aware of the small crowd that had gathered behind them. They were completely stunned, all three of them, and far too interested to feel disappointment or even recall what their original mission had been.

"First arrest I ever saw!" murmured Alison.

"Me too, apart from that phony TV scene," agreed Emmeline.

"Why didn't he use his gun?" was all Jeannie could say. "If he's a *real* policeman?"

The priest who wasn't a priest was just coming to the end of his recital of rights to the woman who wasn't a woman, when a car drew up. Unmarked, but very soon unmistakable.

"Nice work, Jerry!" sang a man's voice from the driver's seat.

"It took you long enough!" said Jerry, giving him a quick scowl. Then he turned back to his prisoner. "Come on, you!" He heaved the prisoner over to the car, the back door of which had now sprung open. "I thought you were supposed to be keeping me in sight," he grumbled, addressing the driver again.

"Yeah, well. Traffic. You know how it is."

Then the front passenger door opened and a woman got out.

"And we were wondering who *else* was keeping you in sight," she said. "Hi, Alison! Emmeline! Jeannie!"

Once again they gaped.

Then Alison blinked and her eyebrows shot up.

"Hey! Angie! Angie Morrison! I—I just didn't recognize you for a second there!"

This was not surprising. At first glance, the young woman who'd stepped out of the car bore not the slightest resemblance to the neat, fresh-faced policewoman they all knew—the friend of Mrs. McNair's, the one that Alison's mother was always holding up to her daughters as a model of tastefulness in dress and make-up.

Right now, Angie looked as if she'd been decked out at Spiderella's Boutique from head to foot—with silver thigh boots, a short leather skirt, a see-through blouse, navy-blue lipstick, and something pearly white daubed on her eyelids.

She closed one of these and laughed.

"Don't mind me," she said. "This is my decoy duty

outfit." Then her face went serious. "But what were you doing, following Jerry? We've had you under surveillance for the past twenty minutes."

"We—I'm afraid we thought he was a phony," said Alison, beginning to feel the keen edge of disappointment at last.

"Ha!" Angie turned to the car. "Hear that, Jerry? These kids spotted you for what you are even if that guy didn't!"

"No, a *crook* phony she means!" said Jeannie.

"Jeannie!" said Emmeline, giving the man in the black hat an uneasy glance.

"Oh?" said Angie, looking at Alison. "How come? What kind of crook would *you* be looking for?"

Hurriedly, they told her, as a uniformed policeman came up and began moving the rest of the crowd along.

Alison suddenly took heart, as she went into details of their quest. She hated to have to seek professional help, after everything she'd had to say about her own detective skills, but maybe Angie could give them some pointers.

But all the policewoman gave at the end of their account was a big stage shudder.

"Now *that*," she said, "is the sort of assignment I would not like. Tracking down that guy in there— Betty Grab-all we call him, he specializes in dressing up as a woman so he can steal their purses without arousing their suspicions—rest rooms, places like that—well, tracking *him* down seemed tough enough. We've been after him for weeks. He's got more wardrobe changes than most real women manage to as-

161

semble in a lifetime. But looking for a credit-card jockey—that's what I call a real Needle-in-the-Haystack job." She frowned. "You say it was someone dressed like Jerry?"

They nodded. Alison fired a suspicious look into the car. She'd just remembered there were such things as crooked cops.

Angie caught her look.

"Hey, now, take it easy, honey!" she said, half laughing. "Old Jerry here's got an alibi. The best. Last week, you said—right? On Monday afternoon? Well, O.K. That was the day he was doing his priest act in the park, right through to six-thirty. I know. I was in the back-up car behind him all the time."

Emmeline was blushing. She cast another glance at the handsome young undercover cop in the car.

"Aw, we didn't really think he'd pull something like that!" she said.

"I'm sure *you* didn't, Emmeline. But Miss Hard Nose here—I'm only kidding, Alison!" The driver was blipping his horn. "Got to be going now," she said, getting back in. "Take care!"

But the policewoman had been wrong. Alison's bitterly morose look had nothing to do with being called "Miss Hard Nose." She'd barely heard it, and, in her role of detective, she'd have found it rather flattering anyway.

No. It was simply her thoughts that had produced the look.

Was nothing *ever* what it seemed in this city? she'd been thinking. So the priest wasn't a priest. Fair enough. But what they had taken to be a *crook* in the disguise of a priest had turned out to be a *cop* in the disguise of a priest. The very opposite. And that was simply shattering.

Alison groaned.

They should smile at an old bleary-eyed drunk who'd mistaken the phony priest for a woman, just because of the long robe! After all this, who was to say *what* the half-blind Corky had glimpsed that other Monday afternoon?

Once again, in the margin of Alison's mind, the shadowy figure began to stoop and straighten, then stoop again and turn and gesture mockingly. . . .

19

Alison Scents the Kill

"Back," said Emmeline, "to Square One!"

They had just entered their squad room, but it wasn't that place that Emmeline was referring to, as she sat down in a heavy dejected lump on the edge of Alison's bed. To her (and this was obvious from the miserable, defeated look in her eyes) Square One was the city of Cleveland.

"I mean let's face it," she said, taking off one of her shoes and easing her toes, "it's Wednesday already. And Daddy says he's had word that J. Hickory Haverstashe might be back tomorrow. Oh, it's hopeless!"

Alison turned from a baleful scrutiny of the pins on the wall map.

"Well, even so, it's another twenty-four hours, Em. And anyway, it's only Thursday tomorrow. I thought you said he wasn't coming back until the weekend?"

Emmeline took off her other shoe and tossed it onto the rug.

"No, well," she said, rubbing that foot, "I guess he

changed his mind. Daddy says he got cornered in the lobby last night. Miss Haverstashe. And while she was yacking on and on about that Easter Parade she's been getting so excited about, she mentioned she'd had a call from her brother saying he'd probably be back Thursday and—Alison!" Emmeline looked up, startled. "Are you listening to me? What—what's the matter with you?"

Alison was making strange gargling noises in the back of her throat. Her head was thrown back and her eyes were wide, showing a lot of the whites. She was frantically flicking the fingers of her right hand, as it waved above her head.

Even Jeannie began to look worried.

Then, out of this apparent trance, Alison began to speak: softly, thoughtfully at first, but with a strong undercurrent of excitement.

"Miss Haverstashe . . . Miss Haverstashe . . ."

"Yes, that's who—"

"In her old raincoat . . . her old dark-blue raincoat . . . down to her ankles nearly . . . And—hey—haven't I seen her in a little black hat, one without a brim, a toque?"

"Yes," said Emmeline, frowning. "She's had it forever. It's about forty years out of date, but—"

"Sure! Sure! And Corky's nearsighted . . . terribly nearsighted. . . . And that drunk back there, saying *Sister* to the "priest." Don't you *see?*" Alison had begun to pace up and down in front of the other two. "Don't you see it could work the other way around?"

"I—I—"

"What are you talking about, Ally?"

165

Alison ignored the fumbling of the older girl and the outright bewilderment on the face of the other.

"The drunk thinks a man is a woman because of the long robe. Right? And the half-blind guy thinks a woman in a long raincoat is a man in a robe. Doesn't that figure?"

"You mean—?"

Now Emmeline was looking very excited again, but Alison paced on.

"And the girl at the boutique . . . yeah!" She smacked her hands together. "Quote—*We get little old ladies too*—unquote. Remember? So why not *big* old ladies?"

Alison stopped and smiled at them—a look of pure triumph on her face.

Then Emmeline sagged slightly. She was looking at the blackboard, just to the side of her friend. She waved a weary hand at the chalked drawing of the credit card.

"Yes. But the card itself, Ally, the card!"

"What? What about the card?"

"With Daddy's name on it."

"Huh?"

"Well, don't you *see?* It's a man's name. You pointed this out yourself. A woman using it would be sure to get challenged."

The glow came surging back to Alison's face.

"Yes, but *is* it?"

She rapped the name with her knuckles.

"Is it what?"

"*Is* it a man's name? Only a man's? How about Dale Evans?"

Jeannie groaned.

"She's a girl!" she said. "She's in my class and I hate her because—"

"Sure, sure, honey! But don't you see, Em? It's a name like—like Dana, and Robin, and Noel, and Alva—and, oh—there's thousands of unisex names like that."

"What's unisex?" said Jeannie, lifting her head sharply.

"Same for both boys and girls, men and women. Hey! And sure! Even the girl in Spiderella's Boutique. Remember *her* name?"

"Gosh!" said Emmeline. "Yes . . . Toni, wasn't it?"

"Right? But what clinches it—listen," said Alison. "Let's go back to the very start of it all. Your father. In a hurry. The florist's. And seeing someone out of the corner of his eye. Someone he didn't want to stop to talk to. A gasbag. A recognized gasbag. Em—" Alison grabbed her friend's arm and yanked her to her feet. *"Right now!* You call your father." She started to drag the girl to the door. "Never mind your shoes. Come into the living room right now and call your father. I want to know just who that person was. Or, rather, I want to *confirm* that information, because I'm darned sure in my own mind."

In a trance herself now, Emmeline allowed her friend to lead her into the McNair's living room. Luckily, the rest of the family were out and the girls had it to themselves. Not that Alison would have been deterred by anyone's presence, now that she was scenting the kill. She lifted the receiver and handed it to Emmeline.

"Dial," she said. "And ask him."

Emmeline dialed.

The other two watched.

"Daddy?" she said at last. "It's me—I . . . Just one thing about the card—no, Daddy, it *is* important. Really . . . When you were in the florist's that afternoon, who was it you saw at the other side of Madison? You know. Who you wanted to avoid? . . . well, *whom* you wanted to avoid then. Honestly, it's important!"

They watched Emmeline's flushed face as she dipped her head, as if to hear better.

Then it jerked up.

"It *was?*" she squealed. "Oh, sorry, Daddy! But—well, thank you!" Alison was plucking at her sleeve impatiently. "That's all we wanted to know . . . no. I can't explain now. Later. 'Bye."

She turned as she replaced the receiver. Her eyes were shining.

"Oh, Ally! You're right! It was Miss Haverstashe!"

"I knew it," said Alison grimly.

"So—?"

"So now we accept that invitation she gave us!"

20
Evidence

"Jeannie seems very quiet today," said Miss Haver-stashe, pouring herself a second cup of tea.

Jeannie stared fixedly back at her for a few seconds, like a kitten when it sees the approach of something strange and possibly menacing. Then she slowly turned and stared at Alison, who frowned slightly and gave her a slow nod, also slight, as if to say:

"That's right. And just be sure to *stay* quiet and you'll be O.K."

For Jeannie had been warned, most severely, as the three of them (all appropriately changed into their most disarmingly girlish dresses: Alison's a dark brownish-greenish plaid, Emmeline's a cornflower blue, and Jeannie's the green velvet with the lace collar) had made their way to Miss Haver-stashe's apartment that afternoon.

"Whatever you do," Alison had said, "don't go blurting it out that we suspect her. Understand? Not until we have absolute proof!"

"But we *know*—"

"We're pretty sure. That's all. But we mustn't let her suspect anything. If she does, it will give her a chance to stall us off. Then she'll get rid of the evidence."

"But—"

"Just leave the talking to me and Emmeline. That will be safest. Just take your cue from us. Then there won't be any danger of you blurting anything out before the right moment. This woman is cunning. And dangerous."

Jeannie had agreed. And for five minutes now she had been sitting there on the very edge of her chair, tense and pale, toying with the glass of milk and the cookie—just wetting her lips with the one and drying them off with the outer crumbs of the other—as if she suspected them to be poisoned.

The other two were putting up a better show. They only sipped their tea, it is true, but that was because it was weak and smelled rubbery and wasn't to their taste. But Alison was on her second cookie, and Emmeline (who was something of a compulsive eater, when under great stress) her fourth. And behind the cover of their cups and cookies, both of the older girls were busy peeking around, hoping to spot enough evidence to enable them to stand up, brush the crumbs off their dresses, and make a firm accusation.

So far, however, they'd not had any luck. The room was crowded with furniture and ornaments, but most of it was big and clumsy and old, like Miss Haverstashe herself, and it seemed to have been de-

signed for much larger premises. Its quality was fairly good, as far as Alison could judge, but it was terribly worn. The couch she and Emmeline were sitting on was a good example. Covered with a once-rich wine-red brocade material, it broke out here and there in little thickets of broken threads, and it too smelled of stale rubber. The carpet on which their feet fidgeted nervously was in a similar condition: once thick and richly patterned, now faded and nearly bald in patches.

"Are you feeling unwell, dear?"

Miss Haverstashe was still addressing Jeannie. The old lady's eyes were bulging behind the glasses with kindly concern.

(And that was another thing, thought Alison. Right from the beginning of their surprise visit, from the immediately warm welcome at the door, Miss Haverstashe hadn't shown a trace of guilt or even shiftiness in her attitude.)

"Huh-hmm!" murmured Jeannie, still staring at her in that tense guarded manner.

Alison looked again from the purplish-tinged face to the plain brown woolen dress the woman was wearing. *That* wasn't new, either, and hadn't been for at least ten years. And it was entirely without decoration, save for the worn leather thong that passed for a belt and gathered up the many folds of cloth. No rings on the old knobby fingers, no watch on the bony wrists. She was still wearing the heavy brogue shoes. Only the lisle hose looked different, no longer sagging and bagging around the ankles, but that could have been a result of the fact that Miss Haverstashe was sitting, knees well bent, rather than to the support of a new garter belt. And, anyway—now that the woman was actually there, before their eyes, it was inconceivable to Alison that she would ever wear anything so gaudy and frivolous.

The Top-flight Fully-automated Girl Detective blinked. All at once she had the sensation of being a plane that had lost height, or a computer that had developed a fault. Had they made a terrible mistake? Now it was she who began to feel guilty.

Miss Haverstashe was still regarding Jeannie with puzzled concern.

Alison pulled herself together.

"It—it's the disappointment over the TV show," she said. "She's never been the same since. Right, Jeannie?"

Jeannie frowned in perplexity as she stared at her sister. Her mouth opened and she formed the word, "What?"

Luckily, Miss Haverstashe had turned to Alison and Emmeline, and missed it.

"Ah yes, my dears!" she said, with a sympathetic crowing noise in her wobbling throat. "I can understand that." She sighed, and the harsh whistling sound was equally sympathetic. "I—I can't tell you how badly I feel for you over that. When everything looked so set for a marvelous career."

There were actually tears in her eyes now. Emmeline fidgeted uncomfortably and reached for another cookie. Alison felt absolutely rotten—so rotten that she was almost on the point of abandoning her line of action. A woman as warm and as full of goodwill as Miss Haverstashe just wasn't *capable* of doing what they suspected her of. Impossible . . .

Then the old lady said something that transformed the whole interview, causing Alison to tingle all over, Emmeline to cough out crumbs, and Jeannie to put her milk down on the battered coffee table with a slam.

"Why," said Miss Haverstashe, giving a sad little nervous gobbling giggle, "you may think this is silly, but I even scraped together enough—I mean I—I even bought a new television set to follow your careers on!"

"Oh?" said Alison, leaning forward, looking around, hoping the others would keep quiet and leave the rest to her.

Miss Haverstashe giggled again.

"Oh, it's not a big one, I'm afraid! Or a color model. It's—" She put down her cup, got up and crossed to the sideboard. Then she opened a door in the massive hunk of furniture, and pulled out something that was its exact opposite: neat, tiny, absolutely modern. "It's one of those cute little Japanese sets," she said, bringing it over.

"Yeah, and we know—"

"Jeannie!"

Just in time, Alison made a grab at her sister's skirt.

"Don't be rude! Sit down! You'll get a chance to look at it!" Then, fighting down the tremor of excitement in her voice, not ready yet for the showdown, Alison said: "Yes, it's a beauty, Miss Haverstashe. And only a twelve-inch screen."

Miss Haverstashe nodded proudly, laying it on the coffee table as if it had been a priceless old vase. Either she was so delighted to possess such an item that all her caution had been forgotten, or it was all just a coincidence. Alison proceeded cautiously.

"But I thought your eyesight wasn't so good, Miss Haverstashe? I mean for an *ordinary* TV set even?"

Miss Haverstashe blinked and slowly turned from her delighted contemplation of the set on the table.

"My eyesight, dear?"

"For watching TV," pursued Emmeline, pushing the last, half-eaten cookie aside. "You said—"

"Ah well, yes," said Miss Haverstashe. "But when one's *friends* are going to appear on TV . . ." She sighed, then shook her head. "What a shame. . . ." Then she brightened a little as she glanced at the set again. "Besides, I find that if I hold it close, like a book almost—well, it's perfectly clear. Wonderfully sharp and clear, these little sets, I find. So much better than a big, expensive one across the other side of the room, like my brother's. I find that terribly blurry. . . . But this must be so embarrassing for you."

She glanced at each of them in turn, as they sat there, squirming, looking at one another, wondering what to do next.

"I mean my little pleasures must seem so trivial compared to the disappointment you've suffered."

She was talking again about their non-appearance on television, and Alison was glad to let her go on, while she herself had another desperate look around.

Then, once more, the tingling.

175

Miss Haverstashe had left the door in the sideboard open. From where she was sitting, Alison could just see the corner of something else that was new, shiny, and out of place in that room.

"Excuse me, Miss Haverstashe . . ."

"Yes, Alison?"

"Is that—in the cupboard there—is that a record player?"

Again Miss Haverstashe giggled—part girlish, part turkeylike—and entirely without guilt.

"Why, yes! What good eyesight *you* have, my dear! You should cherish it. Yes. But it's not a very good record player, I'm afraid. I'd play you some music, but—"

"Don't you have any records—" asked Emmeline, rather too eagerly.

"Yes. I do as a matter of fact. But the only ones I have at the moment are—well—very classical. We should have to sit in perfect silence to do them justice, and I'm sure you girls wouldn't want to do that."

Jeannie was looking hard at Alison. Alison frowned her a cool-it message. The evidence was still not conclusive enough to issue an outright challenge.

To break the uneasy silence, Emmeline said:

"You did say you'd show us the hat you were making."

Afterward, Emmeline admitted that that was the only reason she'd raised the subject. Merely to break the silence. She was a modest girl, and that admission proved it.

Because in fact it gave them just the breakthrough they were looking for.

176

Miss Haverstashe's face lit up. She got to her feet immediately.

"Why, of course!" she said. "Come with me! Now! Come on, come on!" She was leading the way to what turned out to be the bedroom. "It's not quite finished yet, but—"

Alison caught her breath.

Miss Haverstashe had flung open the door with a triumphant flourish, and there, on a sewing table, right in front of their eyes, was revealed the hat.

It was an enormous thing. Basically a black sombrero with a very wide brim, it had had its crown crushed in, or removed completely, or, at any rate, replaced in prominence by a big, pearly-gray ram's horn, laid on its side like a cornucopia. The brim was decorated at the edges with dangling white bobbles; and, scattered about the black felt elsewhere, little jeweled flies sparkled and glittered. There was a crimson silk band, too, around the base of the horn, but it was no ordinary hatband. Alison couldn't be sure at first glance just how the cluster of objects seemingly spilling out from the cornucopia had been fixed in place: the wallet, the watch, the silver cigarette lighter, the gold pen, the small jar of caviar, and so on. But in any case she was too interested in mentally checking off those items on the list she'd been carrying around in her head for the past few days. Also in scrutinizing the big card fixed between the garter-belt hatband and the horn of plenty.

It was roughly the same size as the one she herself had drawn on the blackboard, back in the squad room. But this was much neater. With the use of poster paint and black ink, it was a blown-up but lifelike replica of the object that had caused all the trouble.

NEWCHARGE was emblazoned across the top. Then there was a number, carefully printed, not simply squiggled as on Alison's impatiently drawn mock-up. And at the bottom—well—no—it wasn't Emmeline's father's name. LAUREL C. HAVERSTASHE had been printed there, with a carefully loopy signature below it.

But it—the whole concoction—was evidence enough.

Alison stepped forward, with the others right behind her, one on either side.

21
Confession

"Hey, the ping-pong balls!" cried Jeannie, pointing to the white bobbles. "And the fishing flies! And . . . and . . ."

Now that it was safe for her to speak and nobody tried to stop her, words failed her.

The old lady didn't flinch, didn't frown. She was registering nothing but a happy pride. She was beaming at the three grim-faced girls. She must have thought they were stunned by the sheer cleverness of her handiwork.

"Yes, dear!" she said to Jeannie. "The balls and the flies, they represent the sporting element. I want the theme of the hat to be how useful Newcharge cards can be for all *kinds* of people. Young, old, active, reposeful." She turned to Emmeline. "Don't you think my brother will be pleased, Emmeline? I mean if the hat catches the eyes of the TV news people at the Parade. Think—just *think*—of the advertising, the publicity! Absolutely free!"

But Emmeline was thinking of other matters.

She was staring at the card. Without consulting Alison, without bothering to conceal anything of her pent-up indignation, she pointed at it and, with a sharply accusing note in her voice, said:

"That is a very good likeness of a *real* Newcharge card, Miss Haverstashe!"

The old lady gave a gurgle of delight.

"But of course! It's *meant* to be, my dear. I"—here she did falter a little—"I copied it from a real one."

"I know. My——"

Alison nudged her sharply. There was still a chance that the woman might wriggle out of the net she'd wrapped around herself.

"From your *own* card, Miss Haverstashe?"

"No! My fa——" Emmeline began.

Again Alison had nudged her.

Now Miss Haverstashe looked less pleased with herself. She shook her head.

"No. Not my own card. My brother—he feels— well . . . I've never had a Newcharge card of my own. Or any other kind. My income, you see . . ."

She tailed off.

And this time there was no checking Emmeline.

"You copied it from my *father's* card, didn't you?" Without waiting for a reply, she swung to Alison. "That's the exact number of Daddy's card, Ally! I checked on it and memorized it, after you'd asked me for it the other day." She turned back to Miss Haverstashe. "It's the one my father lost, over a week ago. That's the one you copied it from!"

"Yes," said Alison, feeling there was no point now

180

in pussyfooting around the subject. "And it's the one the finder failed to turn in. And *used* it instead. To buy—oh well!" She gestured at the hat. "Things like ping-pong balls and garter belts and—"

Miss Haverstashe was laughing.

She had thrown back her head until the purple folds of loose, lumpy flesh on her neck were taut and throbbing.

"All right! All right! So my little secret is out!"

"Little?" Emmeline's face was almost as purple as the woman's. Her eyes flashed. *"Little* secret! Why—"

Again Alison nudged her quiet.

"Go on, Miss Haverstashe," she said quite gently. "Tell us about it."

"Of course!" said Miss Haverstashe. "Why not?"

She spoke excitedly at first, giggling in bursts between sentences, telling them how she'd been wanting to catch up with Mr. Grant as he came out of the florist's that afternoon, then about seeing him drop something at the corner, and how she'd picked it up with every intention of returning it to him.

But by the time she'd straightened up, after being buffeted and cursed by some of the passers-by, he had broken away from Rollo and his dogs and was almost at the apartment building.

"Which gave me time to think of this wonderful idea."

"Huh! What's so—"

"Quiet, Jeannie! Go on, Miss Haverstashe."

The woman blinked dubiously for a moment at Jeannie's fierce expression. Then she continued:

"I—I admit that I didn't use the card *entirely* for

181

the hat. I mean—well—I just couldn't resist certain little goodies, things I've always wanted but never been able to—well—afford. But anyway, girls—" She giggled again, her eyes brightening. "It wasn't *stealing,* of course, because as you may know, the company pays, the Newcharge Company, and it will be entirely in their interests if the hat does get shown on television . . . don't you think?"

She gazed around with sudden bewilderment at the three unsmiling faces staring up at her. Then she frowned and, for the first time, a small note of irritability crackled in her voice.

"And anyway," she said, "I'm *entitled* to it! I—I have a lot of my own capital locked up in that business. In—in a way."

"Entitled?" Emmeline blurted. "How can you *say* that, Miss Haverstashe? When my father is likely to —*certain* to—lose his job over it?"

Miss Haverstashe blinked, then looked away and down from Emmeline's face.

"You mean, you think my brother—"

"—will fire Daddy? Yes! And—and we'll have to leave town and go back to Cleveland and—oh—it . . ."

Emmeline's lips were quivering too much to allow her to continue.

"Yes, well," murmured Miss Haverstashe, still looking down at her big, clumsy brogues, "I'll admit I was afraid Hickory might not be so pleased. But I —well—I didn't think it mattered," she said, looking up and keeping her eyes on Emmeline's. "With you being all set to go to Hollywood and all. As—as I

182

thought. I thought your father would be resigning anyway, to help you with the business side of your career—the men in the family always do, don't they? —and—oh, I don't know!"

Suddenly her face seemed to crumple in its purple folds. Her eyes flitted in confusion. She sat down heavily on the bed.

Alison stared at her, at the neat patchwork cover, at the bulky furniture crowding the small room, at the photograph of a man, not young, but much younger than Miss Haverstashe, in a frame on the bedside table. He was dressed in army uniform, and Alison wondered for an instant if it was an old photograph of J. Hickory Haverstashe himself.

"Well, if you have money in the business, Miss Haverstashe, you'll have some say in the matter, won't you?" Alison spoke gently still. She had made up her mind that the old lady really hadn't known just what damage she was doing. Like the Great Detective himself, Alison knew there were times when a cop simply had to make a deal, if only to restrict that damage. "I mean you can use your influence to see that Mr. Grant doesn't get fired," she said, spelling it out. "Can't you?"

Miss Haverstashe wrung her hands and bent her head lower.

"Well—it—it's not exactly like that, you see, dear. I mean when I said I have a lot of capital in the Newcharge business, I didn't mean *money* exactly. I meant—well—it's the same thing really, but—" Suddenly her hands went still. One gripped the other until the knuckles shone almost as white and big as the ping-pong balls. She looked up, and now her eyes were angry. *"Well, I'd say thirty years of one's life were as good as money, wouldn't you?"*

Alison frowned. The others had taken a step back, but Alison could tell that the anger hadn't been directed against them. Even so, she was puzzled.

"I don't understand, Miss Haverstashe. Could you explain, please?"

Miss Haverstashe stared fiercely over their heads.

"Yes," she said. "I will *too!* I don't see why not!" It was as if she were addressing someone else, someone behind them, someone tall and domineering. There was a tremor of fear in her voice as well as anger and bitterness. "I've kept very quiet all these years, but I really do see now that it's the least I can do. I owe it to these girls."

Then she lowered her eyes, blinked, swallowed, and addressed them directly again. Her voice became gentle, weary.

"This," she said, giving the photograph a brief tender stroke with one of her long ugly fingers, "was my friend, my boy friend, the only one I ever had. He was the only one who could ever stand up to Hickory, who didn't approve of boy friends. Jim," she said. She paused. "Lieutenant. United States Marines. Killed thirty-two years ago on Guadalcanal Island."

"That's in—"

"Hush, Jeannie, please! Sorry about that, Miss Haverstashe."

Miss Haverstashe mustered a brief smile for Jeannie.

"Yes, my dear. That's in the South Pacific. I'm—

I'm glad you've heard of it. Anyway"—she gripped her hands hard again—"I got to hear of it on Easter Day, almost exactly thirty-two years ago. And—but that's not what I wanted to say. I wanted to say that Jim and I had planned to take Mother into our home with us, after we were married. She was an invalid even then, you see. I was quite happy to stay home —we lived in Maryland—to look after her. Then . . . well . . . it was sort of expected of me to stick to that plan—even after Jim's death. And—I did. I stayed home with her right to the end." Miss Haverstashe looked up proudly. "Not one day did she ever have to spend in a hospital!" Her head subsided again. "Then three years ago, she died. She was eighty-eight. And I came here, with some of the furniture, to be near my brother."

There was dead silence in that small, stuffy, overcrowded room, as they waited for her to go on.

"So that's what I mean about a lot of capital locked up in the business. You see, I only—*we* only —Mother and I—had what Hickory allowed us. And —well—he isn't the most generous of men. Oh, I know—at first he needed all the money he could get, to build up the business he had then. But even after he'd become very successful, he *still* kept a tight hold on the purse strings. Habit, I guess."

Again a silence.

"Didn't—" began Emmeline. She tried again. "Couldn't *he* have looked after your mother for some of those years, Miss Haverstashe? He *is* married, I know, and—"

"My dear!" Miss Haverstashe gave a harsh, crack-

185

ling laugh. "He's been married three times. That's just *it!* When he was first married, just after the war, he said it wouldn't be fair to a young wife, to saddle her with an invalid mother. And of course I agreed. But as I say, that was three wives ago. So"—she looked up—"can you really blame me—when I found the card—?"

Two tears tracked down the deep folds on either side of her mouth, but she managed a quick brave tusky smile.

Hers weren't the only tears to be flowing.

Emmeline sniffed. Jeannie stole to the side of the old lady and took one of the gnarled hands between her own.

"Don't cry, Miss Haverstashe. *I* don't think you're a horrid perforator any more!"

Alison growled deeply, to clear her throat. She blinked rapidly.

"The—the word's *perpetrator*. And be quiet. I think Miss Haverstashe was going to tell us what she could do—to—to help."

"I'm afraid that my brother," said the old lady, wiping her cheeks with the back of her free hand, "is just a—a—what's that word you kids use, these days?—a—a *crawl?*"

Alison growled again.

"The word you're looking for, Miss Haverstashe, is *creep!*"

The old, sad eyes lit up.

"Exactly, my dear! And I'll be *darned* if he'll fire your father, Emmeline! Just let him *dare!*"

"But—but how can you stop him?"

Miss Haverstashe straightened her back.

"I have an idea. I shall make a clean breast of it to him, the minute he gets back. And I shall demand that he forget the whole thing or—or I shall go to the police and tell them what I've done."

"But—"

"No buts, Alison. That's what I shall do. It is, after all, a criminal offense, *technically*—and they will be forced to charge me with it." She smiled, the yellow teeth bursting out with happy belligerence. "And we'll see how he likes *that!* The family name in all the papers! The sister of J. Hickory Haverstashe, no less . . . Of course, he'll not dare. You'll see."

Emmeline sighed deeply. Her eyes were beginning to brighten, too.

Jeannie released Miss Haverstashe's hand to clap her own.

"Hey, Miss Haverstashe . . ."

"Yes, dear? What pretty hair—"

"What does the J stand for? In J. Hickory Haverstashe?"

"Jeannie!" snapped Alison.

"No, no!" Miss Haverstashe was gurgling with laughter. "A good question, Jeannie. Because that's another thing I'd make sure came out in court, and I'll tell him so. Oh, but he'd never live it down!"

She stamped her feet with glee.

"Yes, but—"

"The J, my dears"—she gasped—"it stands—heh! heh!—for—for *Juneberry!*"

She shrieked with laughter.

"Ju-juneberry?" said Alison, giggling herself.

"Yes! Isn't—isn't it *gorgeous?* You see, our father was a keen arboriculturist. He—he named us both after trees. Laurel Cherry for me, and—ha! ha!— *Juneberry* Hickory for him. And he—ha! ha!—he *hates* it!"

This time it was laughter that bubbled at the springs of the eight tracks of tears, as the three girls and the old lady roared and howled and stamped so hard that even the photograph on the bedside table shook, and so seemed to join in.

22

The Private Showing

Miss Haverstashe was right in her prediction.

She never disclosed to anyone what she actually said to her brother on his return that Thursday. But Mr. Grant came home in the evening to report that he'd never known J. Hickory Haverstashe to be in such a good mood.

"Well, *good* is hardly the right word, I guess," he had added.

Then he went on to explain that it was more of a *quiet* mood. Or a *subdued* mood. And even something of a *considerate* mood. Telling Mr. Grant that he'd heard about the little problem with the missing card, but to forget about it now that it had turned up, to forget *all* about it. Huh?

"And when I went on to tell him I'd already forgotten about it, he seemed very relieved and started talking about the way business was picking up and how there may be a raise for all of us before the year is out."

However, Mr. Grant's memory turned out to be

patchy, once away from the office. Because he did *not* forget who had been responsible for getting him out of the jam. He thanked the girls promptly and fully for all they had done; and when Alison coughed politely and said there was the little matter of expenses, he had responded immediately. Not only did he settle up there and then—after only the briefest of glances at the accounts page in Alison's notebook—but he stood by the promises they had made to their informant.

The very next morning, Mr. Kevin O'Connor was interrupted in his investigations into the contents of a trash basket on Madison. There he was handed an envelope that contained (according to his own estimate) the equivalent of at least twelve months' cash finds, made by no fewer than fifteen full-time expert seekers, in an area of twenty blocks by five, in the palmy days before credit cards had become the curse of his profession.

"Why, bless yez, Kathleen, Adeline and Janet, me darlings, all three! 'Tis a fortune you've given me. With this kinda dough I could take a coupla weeks' vacation in Long Beach, Long Island, and I do believe I will. They say there's still untold riches to be picked up from under the boardwalk there at the height of the season. But of course I'll see that me old pal and business associate Corky gets a percentage of this first."

As for the girls themselves, well, no reward could have been greater than the satisfaction of cracking such a tough case and rescuing Emmeline and her family from the deep trouble they'd been in. All the same, there *was* a bonus—and it was delivered in a strange and unexpected way. . . .

At first sight it looked like a reward for Miss Haverstashe rather than them. She had gone on the Easter Parade that Sunday, escorted by her brother, and her hat had in fact drawn a lot of attention. There had even been a shot of it on one of the late TV news shows, as she had hoped—though it had lasted only a few seconds.

"I could have wished for it to have gone on just a *little* longer," she had complained mildly. "I guess I was sleepy. It was way past my usual bedtime and I wasn't quite quick enough. I'd barely had time to adjust my glasses before the camera had moved to someone else."

"It was a longer appearance than ours, even so!" Alison had commented wistfully.

Then, two days later, Mr. Grant had sprung his big surprise.

The same friend at the network who had tipped him off about the date of the detective episode offered to lend Mr. Grant a videotape of the news program in which Miss Haverstashe and her remarkable hat had appeared. Not only that, he was also willing to lend Mr. Grant a videotape playback machine to go with it.

"It hooks up to a normal TV set, and appears on the screen just like a normal TV program," explained Mr. Grant. "But the great thing is that it can be slowed down or even stopped. I'm sure you'd all like to see your Number One Exhibit at leisure!"

They agreed delightedly, and since Miss Haverstashe's set was far too small, and the Grants' was only black and white, it was decided to use the McNairs' big color set in the living room. Mr. and Mrs. Grant came with the machine, and Miss Haverstashe was invited, and all the McNair family was present, so that there was quite a big audience for this "private showing," as Alison called it. She herself had even put on the sequined denim suit again, because although it wasn't anything like as important to her as the earlier occasion had promised to be, the hat did seem to sum up and symbolize her prowess as a detective.

So the party took place.

Miss Haverstashe was in raptures at being able to gaze at the fruits of her labors for as long as she liked, at such a reasonable hour and in full color; and the only disappointment the girls felt was in the fact that the completed hat loomed so large on Miss Haverstashe's head that it completely blocked out the face of J. Hickory Haverstashe at her side.

"And that was a picture in itself, my dears! The poor boy was trying his best to look cheerful, you know, but it didn't come easy."

Then, as if to change the subject quickly (because, after all, J. Hickory Haverstashe was still his boss), Mr. Grant said:

"And here's another tape I thought you might like to see."

There was a strange twinkle in his eyes.

Suddenly, Alison's heart skipped a beat.

Could it be—?

It was.

It was a tape of the last segment of the Great Detective episode they'd watched with such soaring hopes and plunging spirits a couple of weeks earlier.

"There's the man with the white hat!" squealed Jeannie, all over again.

"And there's the taxi!" murmured Emmeline, gripping Alison's arm.

"And—look out! Here come the police cars!" cried Alison.

It was no use. Even though they knew what had happened before—or what had *not* happened—all their old excitement flared up.

And then, at the critical moment—when the cops drew their guns and the Great Detective stepped forward to make the arrest—Mr. Grant applied the brakes. The picture froze. Behind the Great Detective they saw bushes and the towers of the buildings on Riverside Drive. Mr. Grant pressed a switch. The Great Detective floated on toward the cameras, there was a slight change of angle, a blur in the bushes— golden red and pink—and:

Click!

The picture froze again and the blur took shape, shapes, three shapes—*and there they were!*

Still a little out of focus, but undoubtedly Alison, Emmeline, and Jeannie, rearing up out of the foliage, with the well-practiced looks of horror on two of the faces but something more like demented glee on the third.

But this was no time for carping criticism. Even Tom was silenced. All that mattered was that Alison, Emmeline, and Jeannie were *there,* between the bulky right shoulder of the Great Detective and the brim of

his hat: co-stars, after all, with the flickering screen
to prove it.

"Oh, gosh!" said Alison. "If only we could take an
ordinary photograph of that shot!"

"It's been done, lieutenant!" said Mr. Grant, grin-
ning around at the others, and winking, and producing a large envelope. "Twelve eight-by-ten glossies.
And remarkably clear, considering."

Whereupon the three girls begged to be excused.

They had work to do.

The photographs had to be shared out, and deci-
sions taken.

"We'll have one for the home-room bulletin board, Emmeline," Alison began. "That's top priority. And we'll ask the principal if we can pin one on the main board in the lobby. I can't wait to see Nan Stafford's face when she sees *this!*"

Then she removed the pins from the street map and took it down and, selecting one of the new photographs, set about restoring the Great Detective to his rightful place.

About the Author

E. W. HILDICK is the author of over fifty books for children and teen-agers, seven adult novels, and several critical books. Among his children's books, *Louie's Lot* won the 1968 Diploma of Honor of the Hans Christian Andersen Award Committee as the best children's book to come from Britain in the two years 1966 and 1967. The popularity of his books extends far beyond the English-speaking world. Countries in which his works are enjoyed in translation include France, Italy, Germany, Portugal, Poland, Sweden, Denmark, Holland, Spain, Russia, Yugoslavia, Finland, Norway, Japan, Brazil, and Iceland.

Before he began writing books, Mr. Hildick spent three years as a freelance journalist and short-story writer. In 1957, he won the Tom Gallon Award, one of Britain's most important short-story awards.

As a critic he has written for such journals as *The Times Literary Supplement, The Kenyon Review, Spectator,* and *The Listener.* In 1966–67 he was a reviewer of fiction for *The Listener.*